The Smokies are amazing!

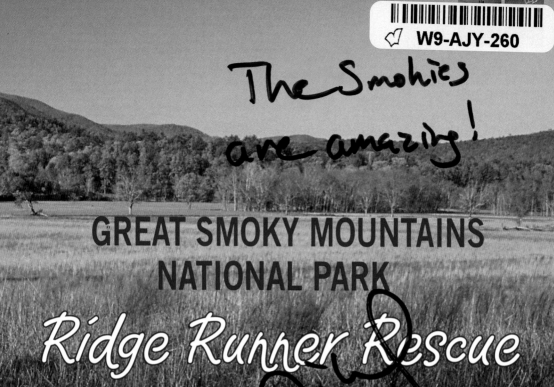

GREAT SMOKY MOUNTAINS NATIONAL PARK

Ridge Runner Rescue

Adventures with the Parkers

Mike Graf

ILLUSTRATED BY
Marjorie Leggitt

FALCONGUIDES

GUILFORD, CONNECTICUT
HELENA, MONTANA

AN IMPRINT OF GLOBE PEQUOT PRESS

FALCONGUIDES®

Photo credits:
Licensed by Shutterstock.com: Title page (all); 1; 3; 5: © Kurdistan; 10; 12: © Tim Mainiero; 13: © BZ Photos; 14; 16-17; 21: © Melinda Fawyer; 22; 23; 25; 29; 30: © Betty Shelton; 38; 41: © Jeffrey M. Frank; 46; 53: © Tim Mainiero; 62–63; 65: © Jeff Kinsey; 66; 70; 71; 77: © Tim Mainiero; 83; 86: © Vahe Katrjyan; 89: © Tim Mainiero; 90; 94 (inside back cover)
© Mike Graf: 11; 24; 26; 31; 43; 54; 59; 70; 78; 79; 82; 88
Illustrations page 73 by Ann W. Douden
Map courtesy of National Park Service

Illustrations: Marjorie Leggitt
Models for twins: Amanda and Ben Frazier

Project editor: David Legere

Library of Congress Cataloging-in-Publication Data is available on file.

ISBN 978-0-7627-7966-6

Printed in the United States of America
10 9 8 7 6 5 4 3 2 1

Hi. I'm Morgan Parker, writing to you from Great Smoky Mountains National Park. Our trip is nearly over, and I can't wait for you to read all about it. It's been quite an adventure.

It's early evening and we're spending the last few minutes of our time here along a "Quiet Walkway." Here's what the sign says about it:

"A short walk on this easy trail offers close-up views, subtle aromas, and the serene quiet of the protected woodland. You will be walking one of the last great wildland areas in the East. But you won't need a backpack or hiking boots. Take your time. Have a seat on a rock or a log bench. This trail has no particular destination, so walk as far as you like and then return."

That's just what we're doing.

Mom is up ahead with her journal, sketching leaves. She really wants to remember the names of as many of the Smokies plants as possible. That's quite a feat because there are so many of them. If I know Mom, she won't forget any of the butterflies and bugs either, like those macaroni-and-cheese-colored centipedes.

Dad is sitting on a bench. His clothes are coated in wet, gooey mud. He's trying to ignore that and instead admire the scenery one last time. I know Dad is amazed at the geology here. He says the Appalachians are some of the world's oldest mountains.

James is over by the river trying to find a few more salamanders. We've seen loads of them and at least a dozen different types. But we still haven't seen the giant waterdog. I think James is hoping for one last chance.

And me? I'm thinking of the things I'll remember most about the Smokies. Like how I got sick while backpacking in the mountains, the women who refused to leave their home when this land was made into a park, the old historic buildings, the streams and waterfalls, and the Appalachian Trail, or AT Trail, as they say here.

But wait, I'm getting ahead of myself.

Right now, above the gurgling, misty river several specks of light just flashed brightly.

When we first saw those we had no idea what they were.

And James just moved closer to the river. "Hey, you guys, come here!" he shouted.

I better go and see what's going on.
Morgan Parker

Dad unfolded the park map.

"It looks like the quickest way out of town and into the Smokies is on this road," he pointed out.

Mom turned onto the side road. Immediately the road steepened. A dense canopy of trees shaded the remote highway.

"*Now* it looks like we're in a national park," James commented.

"We're on the Roaring Fork Motor Nature Trail," Dad said.

The road climbed on. After a while Dad pulled the car over at a turnout, and they all piled out. They walked over to a clearing in the trees with views of the dense, hazy forest covering the rolling hills.

Morgan gazed out. "Now I can see how the park got its name."

"I think," Mom reflected, "the park's natural blue smoke comes from moisture emitted by the plants."

"But some of the haze we see here is also from air pollution," Dad added.

"It looks like a jungle under all those trees," James said. "I wonder what's out there."

"Maybe it's time we find out," Mom suggested.

After driving a short distance, the Parkers loaded up their gear for their first hike. Then they began sloshing up the wet, muddy path. The shadows of the bright green, lacy trees draped over the trail. Birds chirped in the forest. A nearby stream gurgled steadily as it cascaded down the canyon.

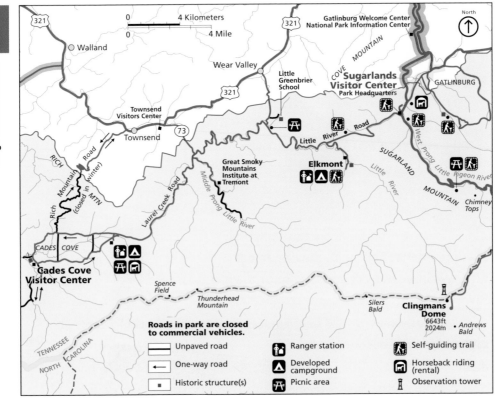

They hiked on. A group of hikers passed the Parkers on their way down. "There's a bear up there," one of the hikers warned.

"Where?" Mom asked.

"About twenty minutes up the trail," the hiker replied. "It was turning over rocks, looking for grubs when we went by."

"Thanks," Dad said. "We'll keep our eyes out."

The Parkers climbed steadily up the rocky trail. Morgan and James scanned the forest as they walked.

Another group of hikers came down.

"At least we got a glimpse of the bear," one of them said to their group.

"But we didn't get to see a hellbender," another replied.

The hikers walked past.

Morgan stopped. "What's a hellbender?"

Dad shrugged. "Don't ask me," he replied with a puzzled look.

The Parkers hiked on, passing trickling wet gullies and small streams. A giant slug slowly crossed the trail.

Dad looked up through a clearing at a massive mountain across the way. "I think that's Mount LeConte. It's one of the sixteen peaks over 6,000 feet in the Smokies. We'll be perched up there soon enough."

"Speaking of perched," Mom whispered, "come here."

Morgan, James, and Dad joined Mom beside a small stream.

Mom pointed to a rock.

"A salamander!" James exclaimed.

James edged closer to the tiny creature. It quickly dashed under the rock. James looked back at his family.

"Sorry," he said.

"The Smokies are the salamander capital of the world," Mom said. "I bet we'll see some more of them."

"I'll keep looking," James announced.

The family hiked on. James and Morgan kept searching for salamanders, while Mom and Dad watched for the bear.

A while later, they crossed over a log bridge and looked up. An arching, feathery veil of water spilled over a cliff and crashed onto the rocks below.

"Rainbow Falls!" Dad said. "We made it."

The Parkers walked up to the falls, sat down, and took out their picnic lunch.

Our picnic view.

After lunch, Mom fished through her backpack. "I think now's the perfect time for my surprise."

Dad looked at Mom. "Surprise?"

Mom pulled out a tattered old book.

"What's that?" James asked.

"My grandfather's—your great-grandfather's—journal," Mom said. "I've been saving it for our trip to the Smokies."

Morgan, James, and Dad looked at Mom and waited for her to explain further.

"He worked here," she said, "for the CCC, or Civilian Conservation Corps, during the Depression. Many young men did park service back then. Grandpa often talked about it when I was a little girl. I remembered his stories when we started planning our vacation here. So I rummaged through his trunk in our attic a few weeks ago and found this."

Mom held up the old journal. "Great Smoky Mountains CCC Days" was inscribed on the cover.

THE CIVILIAN CONSERVATION CORPS

During the 1930s the United States and much of the world experienced a period of time called the Great Depression. People were hungry and out of work. Our president, Franklin Delano Roosevelt, created the Civilian Conservation Corps during this time to employ many of the nation's five million young men who needed jobs. The work was mostly outdoor labor and conservation jobs. These jobs were for unmarried men eighteen to twenty-five years old who had to remain in the CCC camps for at least six months. Their wages were low, and usually more than half of the money the men made went home to their families.

Morgan looked at the journal curiously. "Can we read it?" She smiled and randomly opened the journal. "How about a few pages each day we're here?" Mom suggested.

June 27, 1938

Max Davis here:
I had a day off work today and I sure did need it! Every day the fellas and I haul rocks, build steps, and move and fill dirt to make this trail. The hours are long and hard. But all in all, it's a good job in the beautiful outdoors. And at the end of the day, we have a bed and food. That's a lot more than many folks have these days. Anyway, I hope this trail lasts long into the future so people can appreciate what we've accomplished.
This morning, Freckles, Mop Head, Slim, Jar Head, and I got it in our heads to swim in the Little River. It was cold, but it was great to be clean again! Then we wandered over to an old schoolhouse. Freckles noticed a dirt road nearby, so we followed it. Walking is so easy without our work gear to haul around.
After a bit, we stumbled upon a cabin in the middle of the woods. Much to our surprise, five women were living there. And I thought once this place became a national park everyone was forced to move out. Not these women. They refused to go.
We stayed for a bit and chatted with the gals. They even gave us some apple butter and homemade cornbread for our journey back. Boy, that was a treat.
The Walker sisters is what they call themselves. I'll have to learn more about them. But for now, it's time to hit the hay.

sincerely,
Max Davis
A.K.A. "Bean Pole"

"I can't wait to hear more," Morgan said.
"Me too," Mom replied.

The family packed up and walked down the Rainbow Falls Trail. Morgan abruptly stopped. "Hey, look at these!"

A group of yellow and turquoise butterflies were gathered together on a pile of leaves. They flitted about frantically, with several landing in the pile again.

"They're puddling," Mom said. "That's when butterflies all gather in one place."

Morgan zoomed in her camera and took close-up pictures of the butterflies. "Do you know what kind they are?" she asked Mom.

"The yellowish ones look like swallowtails," Mom answered. "I'll have to look at your pictures and my book later to identify the turquoise ones. But they sure are pretty."

The Parkers walked on.

A few minutes later, Dad stopped. "Whoa!" he called out.

A long black snake was gliding across the path. The snake slithered along, flicking its tongue in and out of its mouth, then quickly disappeared into the bushes.

"A black racer," Mom said. "Beautiful!"

"If we missed the bear, at least we got to see a snake," James said.

The Parkers eventually made it back to the car. They climbed in and continued driving along the Roaring Fork Motor Nature Trail.

They drove up to an old cabin.

"Pretty unusual to see that in a national park," Dad said.

Dad pulled over and parked the car at the Ephraim Bales Place. A path led up to the old log home, and it had two rock chimneys.

The Parkers got out and gazed at the structure. James read the information sign.

"Eleven people lived in that house!" he exclaimed.

"That must have been snug," Mom said.

PIONEER PLACES

The Great Smoky Mountains has one of the best collections of log buildings in the eastern United States. Almost eighty historic structures, including houses, barns, churches, schools, gristmills, and other buildings, have been preserved in the park. The best places to see them are at Cades Cove, Cataloochee, Oconaluftee, and along the Roaring Fork Motor Nature Trail.

The Parkers walked inside the cabin. James peered out of the only window in the house. "There's another building out there," he noticed. The Parkers walked outside while Morgan took several pictures. "That must be the corncrib," Mom said of the other structure.

They walked back to their car, passing the yellow, blue, and green Alfred Reagan Place.

"I could live in a home like that," Dad stated.

"It does look much more modern and kept up," Mom replied.

Soon they approached an area of large, mossy boulders. Small branching waterfalls cascaded down in between the rocks.

"This must be the Place of a Thousand Drips," Morgan announced.

Dad pulled over and parked the car. The Parkers stared at the series of mesmerizing waterfalls.

As the family stood there, Morgan pulled out her journal and wrote.

Dear Diary,

I've been to several national parks before, but so far nothing at all like the Great Smoky Mountains. There are so many unusual things about this place. James and I really want to see more salamanders. And what is a hellbender anyway? But I think what we're most interested in are the old buildings. What are they doing here—and what happened to all the people who used to live in them? I hope we'll find out as we spend more time here.

More soon, I promise!

Morgan

A thousand-drip waterfall.

Mom looked at her family. "It's time to climb!" she announced.

"And without having to haul a ton of gear," Dad added.

"It's kind of a novelty hiking to the only overnight lodge in the park," Mom said.

"And apparently it's a pretty famous place. I had to make the reservation a year ago," Dad added. "It was built in 1930, before the Smokies became a park."

It was a cloudy day, and the Parkers were on the Alum Cave Trail. They headed toward the Mount LeConte summit, five-and-a-half miles ahead.

The beginning of the trail followed a gurgling stream with a wisp of mist hovering above it. Morgan and James glanced at the water often, hoping to get a glimpse of more salamanders.

Ahead, a series of stairs led through a massive slab of rock. "That must be Arch Rock," Dad announced. He gripped a cable and led his family up the wet stairs.

Dad waited at the top and looked down through the rock formation. Morgan reached Dad first. "It's kind of like going through a cave," she said.

Mom and James caught up, and they all climbed on.

Soon the trail came to a rocky point with purple flowers blossoming in the nearby bushes. "These are the rhododendron the park is famous for," Mom announced.

Morgan examined one of the shrubs. "They look like the type of flowers we have in our yard."

Mom studied the purple petals too. "You're right!"

A while later, the Parkers approached a massive overhanging rock protecting the trail underneath it. Dad led the family up some wooden stairs and underneath Alum Cave Bluff.

James felt something land on his head. He looked up. "There's water dripping down from underneath the top of the rock!"

After a few minutes at Alum Cave Bluff, the Parkers climbed on. The trail passed more mossy, wet areas with cables along the side for gripping.

"You know," Dad commented, "Mount LeConte is 6,593 feet high. That means it's one of the highest mountains in the park, and in all of the Appalachian Mountains, for that matter."

James took a deep breath and rested a moment. "I can tell."

Morgan, James, Mom, and Dad trudged on. The trail leveled out for a time, and the family got their first view of the bulging summit ahead.

"We still have to climb all that!" James exclaimed.

Raindrops started plunking down, and thunder rumbled in the distance. Mom broke out rain parkas and handed them out. They put on their colorful rain gear and forged ahead.

"Look!" James announced.

On the base of a mossy tree was a tiny orange salamander. It clung to the trunk and stayed motionless as the Parkers inspected it. Morgan zoomed in her camera on the beautifully colored amphibian and took several photos.

They're so cute.

"It's the same color as your parka," James said to Dad.

Eventually they approached the final ascent. Trees alongside the trail were stunted and moss-covered. The Parkers held on to the cables and pulled themselves up as the rain started pelting down harder.

They reached the top of the trail. "Let's hurry to the lodge and check in," Mom suggested as she sloshed through a puddle.

Up ahead was a series of rustic wooden cabins.

Morgan, James, Mom, and Dad walked up some stairs and into the lodge's office.

Dad told a woman behind the counter about their reservation. After checking the Parkers in, she looked at the rain pouring down outside. "It looks like you got here just in time," the woman commented.

WILDFLOWER NATIONAL PARK

More than 1,500 species of flowering plants grow in the Smokies. Because of that, some people have nicknamed the park Wildflower National Park. From mid-April to mid-May, spring wildflowers such as columbine, trillium, and lady slipper orchids bloom in forests before the trees grow leaves and shade the forest floor. From mid-June to mid-July, beautiful displays of mountain laurel, rhododendron, and azalea are common, especially at higher elevations. The Smokies has annual guided wildflower walks and talks every spring.

The Parkers hurried to their cabin. It was a small room with two double-sized bunk beds covered with colorful woolen blankets. There was a desk next to the bed, with a lamp on it.

Mom looked at the rustic surroundings. "It's quite charming in here."

Dad plopped down on the lower bed and fished through his day pack. He pulled out his book and listened to the rain's steady drone on the roof. "I guess the weather is telling us what we're going to do for the rest of the day."

James climbed onto the upper bed, and Morgan followed him.

Mom lay down next to Dad. "How about hearing another page from Great-Grandpa's journal?" she suggested.

"Can you read another page about the Walker sisters?" Morgan asked.

Mom thumbed through her grandfather's journal. "Here's one."

September 2, 1940

Max Davis here:

It seems that the only chance I get to write is on a day off work. Well, today was one of those days, and I witnessed history.

Franklin Delano Roosevelt, our 32nd president, gave a speech at Newfound Gap, right next to the Appalachian Trail I've been working on. In his speech, he dedicated the park to all people now and in the future. It was a grand occasion, and thousands of people were there to witness the event.

This certainly is a great national park. Just the AT itself is worth seeing. By the time I'm finished here, we'll have helped establish seventy miles of incredible hiking in the park.

My buddies from camp and I have visited the Walker sisters several times now. They are some of the only people left in the area now that it's a national park. And it's quite a home they're living in. Newspaper and magazine clippings are all over the walls and all kinds of objects are stored on shelves and hanging from nails hammered into the wooden ceiling.

They also have a beautiful garden with fruit trees and vegetables. There were a couple of rabbits running around out there. Margaret shooed them away and even threatened that she would get the rifle if they came back. I guess the rabbits are eating out of the garden.

They showed us this wooden storage structure they built right over some water that was diverted from the creek. The water keeps things cool and fresh, just like an icebox.

Anyway, Freckles asked Louisa if he could use the bathroom. Well, Louisa got all red in the face and giggled and said something that surprised us all.

"There is no bathroom." Then Louisa nodded and pointed to the woods.

Freckles walked sheepishly into the forest, out of sight, just like the Walker sisters do.

Anyway, I shall close for today.

More from the Smokies soon,
Max Davis

Later that afternoon, Mom got up. "Does anyone want to go check out the lodge?"

Morgan got out of bed and scratched the back of her head. "That sounds good to me."

The family put on their rain parkas and walked over to the office. Once inside, they looked around at the displays on the walls. Dad found the precipitation totals on Mount LeConte. "Let's see," he said, "this chart shows moisture received each year: 75 inches, 77, 80, 92, 100, and 62. That's quite a lot of rain and snow!"

James found an article on a famous LeConte climber. "Ed Wright made his 1,281st trip up here in 2004. And he was seventy-eight years old!" he announced.

Mom looked at Morgan and James. "Well, you two have only 1,280 trips left to catch him, and sixty-eight years to do it!"

Morgan smiled. "That's if he hasn't climbed up here since then."

James did some quick math in his head. "If Morgan and I climb Mount LeConte twenty times a year for the next seventy years, we'll each have been up here 1,400 times."

Dad laughed. "Keep me informed on your progress, would you?"

Morgan studied a map on the wall, then turned toward her family. "These tacks show where Mount LeConte visitors have come from." She started naming some of the places marked by tacks. "New York, Phoenix, Los Angeles ..."

The rest of the family joined Morgan. "None from San Luis Obispo, California," James realized.

"Until now," Dad said. He pulled a spare tack from the wall and handed it to Morgan.

Morgan took the tack and pushed it in on San Luis Obispo. "Now we're on the board too," she said proudly.

Mom glanced out the window. "I think it stopped raining."

"We can head out to see the sunset," Dad suggested.

They grabbed their belongings and splashed up the trail to the cliff tops.

Other visitors were also at Mount LeConte's viewpoint, watching the hazy sun sink behind distant, rounded mountains.

The family looked out at the view. "I can see our trail way down there," James announced.

Then the Parkers heard the sound of a rotating motor approaching.

A helicopter appeared out of the fog. It hovered a short distance away from Mount LeConte's summit.

"It looks like it's trying to land," Morgan said.

A moment later the helicopter maneuvered closer to the ground until it was out of sight behind some trees.

"I can still hear it," James reported.

"I wonder what it's doing up here," Morgan pondered.

A big, dark cloud drifted overhead. Quickly the top of Mount LeConte was enveloped in an eerie, wet mist. Even some of the treetops faded away into the fog.

The helicopter sounded like it was lifting. Quickly it was above the trees again. "There it is!" James called out.

Then lightning flickered. It was instantly followed by cracking, booming thunder. The helicopter flew away and disappeared into the clouds.

"Time to head back!" Mom announced.

The Parkers dashed down the wet trail. Rain started pelting down and soon turned to hail. Pea-sized balls of ice bounced all around and started to accumulate.

By the time they reached their cabin, ice completely covered the ground. Morgan, James, Mom, and Dad hurried inside. They hung up their wet clothes, and Mom lit the kerosene lamp.

Dad turned the propane heater up. "There's no place like home," he said.

Soon Morgan and James were in bed reading while rain and hail pelted down loudly on the cabin's roof. Mom leaned her head next to Dad's. "It's quite a ruckus out there," she said, "but we all look so comfortable in here!"

Morgan sat up and scratched the back of her head. She felt around her neck and hair. "Yuck!" Morgan yelped. "I can feel something crawling on me, but I can't get it off!"

Dad hopped up. "Where?"

Morgan moved her hand away. "I see it," Dad announced.

"What is it?" Morgan asked nervously.

"A tick," Dad responded, "near the base of your neck."

Mom rushed over. "A tick?"

Morgan climbed down from the bed.

Dad got a napkin and slowly moved in on the tick. "Hold still," he directed Morgan.

"I can still feel it moving!" Morgan squealed.

"Not for long," Dad said. He zeroed in further and squeezed the napkin around the tick. Dad held the tick out for Morgan and the rest of the family to see.

The green-and-brown-spotted insect was upside down with its juices squeezed out. Its legs still kicked around slowly. "Eeew," Morgan squeaked. "That thing was on me?"

"And it's still alive," James informed her.

Dad crushed the tick.

Mom moved Morgan's hair around and got a good look at Morgan's head and neck. "All gone," she said. "But I'm going to clean that area with antiseptic, okay?"

The Parkers began checking themselves for ticks. James found one on his sock. Dad got rid of one on his pants. They inspected each other's hair and clothing. "I think we're all clear for now," Dad announced.

Dad straddled his bicycle while looking at Mom, Morgan, and James. "Is everyone ready?"

"Ready!" the rest of the family replied.

The Parkers peddled away from the bike rental shop and headed toward Cades Cove. They made a quick left turn and entered the historic eleven-mile stretch of road.

"It's great to be out here when no cars are allowed," Morgan commented.

They quickly came to a view of all of Cades Cove.

"Now I know why this place is so popular," Mom said. "It's beautiful."

James walked up to the barbed wire fence separating the Parkers from the fields and meadows.

"I wonder," James thought out loud, "if this fence is to keep the wildlife in, or us out?"

Dad laughed. "Speaking of wildlife, do you see what's out there?"

Morgan, James, and Mom scanned the fields. "Over there," Morgan pointed. "A wild turkey."

"One of several," Dad said. "There are two more that way."

The Parkers rode on and quickly came to a short path leading to the Oliver Cabin. They leaned their bikes on a fence and walked up to the picturesque old home.

James read the information sign. "This home was built in the 1820s," he called out. "It's one of the oldest homes in the park."

"It sure is in good shape, then," Mom said.

The Parkers walked around the log cabin. They went inside and examined the first floor before climbing up to the loft. Then they went back outside. "This is quite a house," Morgan said while holding onto one of the wooden poles supporting the cabin's porch roof.

They walked back to their bikes and pedaled along farther. The road was mostly flat but dipped up and down some small rolling hills. "Wait up!" Morgan called out while huffing her way up a hill.

Dad stopped for Morgan. "These one-speed bikes are difficult to pedal, aren't they?"

"Yes," Morgan said between breaths.

The Parkers passed an old church with a cemetery next to it. A few minutes later, they stopped at another clearing.

Morgan pointed. "Hey, look! There's four deer out there!"

"That makes four deer and three wild turkeys," James said.

Mom laughed. "And no salamanders today."

A few minutes later, the Parkers stopped at a side road. "I wonder what that's for?" Morgan said.

James looked at his map. "I think that's where the Abrams Falls Trail is. Can we go?"

"Absolutely," Mom answered. "But I think it's best to drive out here later so we don't get caught on our bikes in traffic."

Mom looked at her watch. "It's almost 9:30," she announced. "In thirty minutes they open the road to cars."

"And we're not even halfway done yet," James added.

"Better get a move on, then," Dad said.

Morgan, James, Mom, and Dad kept riding. They stopped briefly at the visitor center to mill around. Mom bought a book on Great Smoky Mountains history. The family finished the rest of the loop just as several cars caught up to them.

A herd of deer was grazing on the lawn next to the bike shop. "Hey," James called out, "we didn't even have to go into Cades Cove to see wildlife."

"But I'm glad we did," Dad responded.

The Parkers returned their bikes and had lunch at their nearby campsite. Morgan lay down in the tent after lunch. *I've got a stomachache,* she realized, *and I feel weak.*

Mom peeked in a bit later. "Are you ready for the hike up to Abrams Falls, honey?"

Morgan took a deep breath and slowly sat up. "I'll be there in a minute."

The Parkers drove back into Cades Cove and pulled into the Abrams Falls parking lot.

Morgan, James, Mom, and Dad tromped along the wet, rocky trail.

Dad looked up at the darkening sky. "I think it's just about to rain again."

They put on their parkas just as the rain hit. "The climate is so fickle here," Mom commented. "From one minute to the next, it's always changing."

Dad smiled. "That reminds me of an old saying about the weather in New England: 'If you don't like the weather, wait a minute.'"

"That means," Morgan added, "that it probably won't be raining in a minute."

"Probably so," Mom agreed.

They tramped through the rain, splashing in and around puddles. James kept searching for salamanders in nearby seeps and small streams.

All of a sudden it got really dark. Thunder rumbled in the distance. Then the clouds let loose. Rain poured down on the Parkers, but they hiked on anyway.

A beautiful waterfall.

A few minutes later, the rain did let up. The sky brightened, and the sun tried to peek through the clouds. Then the rain completely stopped.

"It's too warm for these now," Mom said while shedding her parka. Morgan, James, and Dad took theirs off too.

The Parkers turned a bend on the trail. Straight ahead of them was a wide, multitiered cascade of water tumbling turbulently into a large pool.

"Abrams Falls!" Dad announced.

The Parkers walked closer to the falls. Along the way they passed an isolated pool of water.

James bent down to inspect the pool more closely. "You guys, come look at these!"

Hundreds of pollywogs were swimming around in the stagnant water.

"One of the many life-forms in the Smokies," Mom remarked. "A bunch of them already have legs," she observed. "They'll be metamorphosing into frogs soon."

By now, the cool, wet weather had turned warm and humid. Even the rocks were dry enough to sit on, so the family sat down near the falls. Dad looked around at their surroundings. "Do you know the Cherokee legend about this place?"

"What?" James asked.

"It goes something like this," Dad began. "A buzzard was flying over the area for a long time. It got tired of flying, and its wings dropped down and touched the ground, forming valleys. When its wings came up, they formed the mountains."

"Well, it sure is pretty here," Morgan said. Then she looked at her family. "How about a group picture?"

Morgan lined everyone up so that the falls were behind them. She placed her camera on a rock and set the automatic timer. Morgan clambered over to join her family just as the camera clicked.

Morgan showed the picture to James, Mom, and Dad.

Suddenly, thunder rumbled in the distance. "It looks like our little picnic is just about over," Dad called out.

The family packed up and put their parkas back on just as the rain started coming down. Then they began their two-and-a-half-mile walk back to the car.

The Parkers were on a long drive from Cades Cove to Cataloochee.

Mom was driving.

"I think I'll write in my journal now," James announced.

This is James Parker reporting.

We are in Great Smoky Mountains National Park—the largest national park in the United States east of the Mississippi River. There are no entrance stations at this park. That's because the people of North Carolina and Tennessee who donated the land wanted it to be free for people to enjoy forever.

We've seen a bunch of salamanders. If you ever come here, just hang out by a small creek or stream, be still, and keep looking around. I almost guarantee you'll see one. A type of salamander we haven't seen is the hellbender. When I first heard that name, I didn't know what it was. We found out that it is the largest salamander in the park and grows over two feet long!

We just stopped at Oconaluftee Visitor Center to see the Mountain Farm Museum and Mingus Mill. They started grinding corn at the mill in 1886, and they still do it to-day. The mill was also one of the first buildings the CCC helped restore in the park. Now there are volunteers working there to teach people like us how it works. Because of that, we got a good idea of how the early settlers prepared food around here. Dad even bought a Smokies recipe book for us to try out at home. Mmmm...

Anyway, I know I'll have much more to report soon from the Smokies!

Sincerely,

James Parker

Dad heard James close his journal. He turned back to look at the twins. "I just found another entry about the Walker sisters," he reported. "Do you want to hear it?"

"Yes!" Mom, James, and Morgan answered eagerly.

July 22, 1938

Max Davis here:

Guess what I did again today? I visited what is nicknamed Five Sisters Cove, where the Walker sisters live.

I learned that several years ago, there were six of them there. But in 1931, Nancy died because of asthma and breathing problems that she had dealt with all her life. Life out in the woods can't be easy.

Louisa told me she wants to be a writer. She's been jotting down poems about her mountain life. One of the poems she calls "My Mountain Home." she says she's still working on it, but with her permission, I copied down a few of the verses.

My Mountain Home

There's an old weather bettion house
That stands near a wood
With an orchard nearby it
For almost 100 years it has stood.

It was my house in infency
It sheltered me in youth
When I tell you I love it
I tell you the truth

But now the park commissioner
Comes all dressed up so gay
Saying this old house of yours
We must now take away.

So far, the Walker sisters haven't left. The park service tried to get them to leave like all the other families, but they refused to go.

Dad closed the journal.

"Well, now we know how Louisa felt about this becoming a park," Mom commented.

"I wonder if people will read our journals when we're older," James mused.

The Parkers drove through historic Cataloochee Valley, passing some old homesteads, a school, and a church. As they approached the end of the road, Morgan, James, Mom, and Dad noticed other visitors gazing at the fields.

James pressed his hands against the window and stared out. "I wonder what they're looking at."

Mom pulled over and parked the car.

The Parkers walked up to join a small crowd of people.

"Look out there!" James exclaimed.

A herd of female elk was grazing about.

James started counting. "There are six of them," he announced.

Dad looked all around. "There's a bull elk, off in the distance."

Suddenly another bull elk pranced out of the forest. It arched its neck, opened its mouth, and bugled loudly. Then it put its antlers down and trotted over to the other male.

The two males looked at each other and then charged, locking their antlers. They pushed and shoved each other back and forth. After several minutes, one of the elk ran away.

Morgan looked at Mom. "Did they hurt each other?"

"It seemed like they were just sparring to get ready for the rutting season," Mom replied. "That's when the males battle it out for the females."

"Yeah, the big action will be in the fall," Dad added.

The family watched the female elk graze while one of the males stood close by. The hazy, smoky air cooled as the sun slipped below the hills. Morgan snapped several photos.

Mom sighed. "I guess we better go get our campsite now."

The Parkers piled back into the car and drove to the campground for the night.

• • •

The next morning, the Parkers were back, exploring Cataloochee Valley.

They approached the old school and noticed tons of cars parked there and by the nearby chapel. Around the side of the church, tables were set up with all kinds of food. James noticed the dessert. "Apple pie!" he exclaimed. But there was also fried chicken, potato salad, deviled eggs, green beans, and other dishes.

"Looks like they're getting ready for a feast!" Mom exclaimed.

A woman near the front of the church started speaking to the people gathered around. Morgan, James, Mom, and Dad stood off to the side and listened.

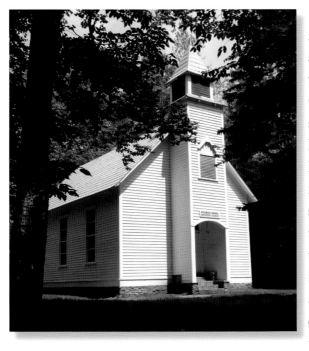

"Welcome to another reunion of the family and friends of those who once lived in the Cataloochee area. I can see the Caldwells, Messers, Hannahs, Woodys, and Palmers here, and many, many others. It's great to see all of you back visiting the park again! As usual, we have some of our favorite foods to feast on and traditional Appalachian music to get our toes tapping. So thank you all again for coming, and dig in…That food is fixin' to be eaten!"

The crowd let out a holler, then people began to make their way toward the buffet.

"I wish *I* was from here!" James commented while eyeing the food.

The Parkers watched for a moment. "We should probably go," Mom said. "I feel like we've invaded someone's private party."

Morgan, James, Mom, and Dad walked away from the church and headed into the white schoolhouse.

The schoolroom was full of desks in rows of four. An old chalkboard was at the front. The family sat down in the first and second row. Morgan looked around. "Wow. Schoolrooms sure have changed," she said.

James spontaneously stepped to the front of the class and faced his family. "Okay, everyone," James spoke like a teacher. "It's time to get ready for your next lesson."

Dad egged James on. "Show us what you've got!"

James tapped on the chalkboard with a pretend piece of chalk. "It's afternoon now," teacher James instructed, "and that means it's time for math." He stared at his three pupils.

Mom, Dad, and Morgan looked up at James for further instructions.

James scanned the whole classroom, imagining it was fully occupied. "Okay, I see that you're all ready," James smiled. "Well, today we're learning long division."

Using his fingers, James wiped dust off the chalkboard and traced out 1,075 divided by 6. Then James started explaining the problem. "The six goes into the ten, once, and…"

"School on our vacation, yuck!" Morgan muttered to herself.

"One times six is six. Put the six under the ten and subtract. That gives you four. Now bring down the seven and…"

Morgan stopped paying attention to the pretend lesson. She put her head down on the desk and pictured herself in this very same classroom, many years ago.

Children were piling into the schoolhouse from outside, wearing old-fashioned clothes. The girls were all in long dresses. Morgan sat straight up. Six girls of various ages found desks nearby.

"I see you're new here," one girl said. "Let me tell you what to expect."

"Okay," Morgan nodded.

"I'm Margaret," the girl explained. "Since it's afternoon, we'll be learning math right away. But that's not all we do. The morning is for writing, spelling, and grammar. And later today we'll do some handwriting. Oh—and I hope you're ready for Parents' Day tomorrow. It's Friday, and we're having a spelling bee!"

"A spelling bee?!"

"Yes, with all of our parents watching!"

"Really?" Morgan sat up anxiously.

"Can you spell Cataloochee?"

"C-A-T-A-L-O-O-C-H-E-E," Morgan spelled carefully in her mind.

"Excellent!"

Morgan noticed the six girls had similar-styled dresses on.
"Are you all sisters?"

"Uh-huh," Margaret replied. "We're the Walker sisters. This is Nancy, Martha, Polly, Louisa, Hettie, and I'm Margaret." She introduced her five sisters while each of them nodded.

"Nice to meet you," Morgan said. She noticed Margaret's lunch basket. "What do you have in there?"

"Oh, cornbread, jam, and..." Margaret reached into her bag and pulled out a large red, ripe apple. "An apple a day keeps the doctor away, you know!"

Morgan heard three taps on her desk. She quickly sat up. James was standing next to her trying to look serious. "Are you paying attention, young lady?" he asked, then started laughing.

Morgan smiled at her brother.

Mom looked at Morgan and James, then stood up. "I think school's out for the day. And all of us are excused."

"Yeah!" James called out, quickly sounding like a ten-year-old again.

The Parkers ambled back outside. "Come on," Dad said, "I want us to see a couple more things around here."

Dad drove the family toward the historic Palmer House. They examined the small museum's artifacts from the area and listened to the recordings about pioneer and Native American life.

Afterward, they walked to the nearby cemetery.

An elderly woman was putting some plastic flowers on a grave site. She bent down and pushed the flowers into the ground. Then the woman quietly spoke to the grave. She slowly stood back up and gingerly made her way back down the hill, passing the Parkers along the way.

The cemetery had a number of tombstones. Some were small, some large, and some adorned with flowers. The Parkers walked around, reading the engravings.

"Here's a child who only lived for two years!" James called out.

"She was just a baby," Mom commented.

"And here's an eight-year-old who died," Morgan said.

"Pioneering in these mountains was a hard life," Dad reflected. "Until vaccines were discovered, it was not uncommon for young children and adults to die from diseases that we no longer have to worry about."

Mom walked up to a tombstone. "Here's a woman who lived a *long* time."

Dad stepped over and looked at the dates on the tomb. "Hey, Mr. Math," Dad called out, "this person was born in 1839 and passed away in 1931. So how old was she when she died?"

James stopped walking and thought for a moment.

"Ninety-two!" Morgan blurted out.

"Correct!" Mom said proudly.

Later that day, the Parkers drove the back roads between Cataloochee and Cosby. The gravel road skirted the park border and the forest.

After the scenic drive, they arrived at Cosby campground. James, Morgan, Mom, and Dad set up camp. Then Dad lay back on the bench of the campsite's picnic table and stared at the jungle of trees above.

Morgan and James also looked up. "There are so many leaves, I can barely see the sky," Morgan said.

As dusk approached and the evening slowly cooled, Dad started a fire. They all sat around, eating toasted marshmallows. "We'll miss this on the trail," Mom mentioned as she gobbled up a singed treat.

James stood up. "I'm going to the bathroom."

"Me too," Morgan added.

James looked at Mom and Dad. "We'll be right back."

Morgan walked over to the sink to wash her hands. She looked up. There were a bunch of large moths clinging to the wall.

Each moth was different. One was small, the size Morgan expected moths to be, with

light, translucent yellow wings. Several medium-sized moths had interesting patterns of color on their wings.

Morgan gazed at another moth closer to the ceiling. *That one is tiny,*
she thought. Morgan stood on her tiptoes and studied the moth. It was
peach-colored, with an orange-yellow head and miniature red antennas.

Morgan heard a loud knock. She jumped back from the wall.

James called out from the men's room, "Morgan, are you there?"

"Yes," Morgan answered, trying not to be too loud.

"You have to see these moths!" James shouted.

"Meet me outside, okay?" Morgan replied.

James and Morgan dashed out of the bathrooms and nearly ran into
each other. "One's huge and it's colored funny," James blurted out. "The
lower half of its wings are light gray and see-through. The top part is
orange and white, like a butterfly. Do you want to come and look?"

Morgan took a step back. "I'm not going in there. Besides," she
added, "there are interesting moths in my bathroom too." Morgan
smirked at her brother. "Do *you* want to come and look?"

"No!" James replied.

"I've got an idea," Morgan called out. She grabbed James's arm and
led him quickly toward camp. Mom and Dad were sitting by the fire.
Dad was reviewing the park map and a hiking book. Mom was reading
a chapter from *It Happened in the Great Smokies,* a book with stories of
the events and people that helped make Great Smoky Mountains National
Park. Mom looked up. "You two were gone quite a while."

Morgan opened the car door and started frantically searching. She
stood up and looked toward Mom and Dad. "Have you seen my camera?"

"I think it's in the glove box," Dad replied.

Morgan found her camera then looked at James. "Come on, let's go."

"Go where?" Mom inquired.

"There are these incredible moths in the bathrooms," Morgan
informed her parents. "We're going to take pictures."

Mom looked at Dad. "Interesting," she stated. "Just don't disturb the moths, okay?"

Morgan and James dashed back toward the bathrooms.

A few minutes later they came trotting back. "You guys have to see these!" James announced.

Morgan flipped through pictures of the moths on her digital camera.

"I really like the small one with the soft, yellow wings," Dad commented. "But they're all beautiful."

Mom smiled. "I believe we have two budding entomologists on our hands. Insect scientists in the family: I love it!"

Dad drove to the nearby overnight parking lot.

A white van with a Great Smoky Mountains Shuttle logo on it drove up. "There's the ride to our backpack on the Appalachian Trail," Mom announced.

Morgan, James, Mom, and Dad threw their packs into the back of the van and piled in.

"Are you the Parkers?" the driver asked.

"That's us," Mom replied.

The shuttle driver turned down the road leading out of Cosby.

A while later, the driver looked into her rearview mirror and spoke. "Did you hear about that rescue near Mount LeConte the other day?"

Dad looked up. "Rescue?"

"Yes," the driver reported. "Apparently a guy got seriously injured and couldn't hike on. A Ridge Runner, a person who patrols the AT Trail, had to radio for help."

"What happened to him?" Morgan asked.

"I heard he had to be helicoptered out. It was a life-threatening situation."

"So that's why we saw the helicopter up there!" James exclaimed.

Morgan took a deep breath. "Is he okay now?"

"I'm not sure," the driver answered. "I haven't heard any more news. But I did hear it was touch and go for a while."

The Parkers gazed at the scenery along Highway 321, which borders the park. They passed back through busy, touristy Gatlinburg.

Soon they were on Newfound Gap Road. Eventually the van driver turned toward Clingmans Dome and headed for the park's highest peak.

At the end of the road the Parkers grabbed their food and small packs and said good-bye to the driver.

"See you at one o'clock," Dad called out.

The driver gave Dad a thumbs-up signal and nodded her head. "You got it!"

Mom led the way on a 1.8-mile wet, sloshy trail to Andrews Bald.

The trail wove through a dark, mossy forest. Morgan gazed into the mysterious woods. "Where are the gnomes?"

Dad laughed. "It does look like a perfect place for them, doesn't it?"

James turned toward Mom. "What's a bald?"

"I was wondering that myself," Mom replied, "so I looked it up in our guidebook. Apparently there are a few open areas on the tops of ridges here. Andrews Bald is one of them."

The Parkers hiked on. A short while later, the dense thicket of trees gave way to an open field of grasses, wildflowers, and small bushes.

"I guess this is a bald," Dad said.

Mom walked toward some small boulders in the grass. "This looks like a good spot for a picnic," she announced.

Dad reached into his backpack, pulled out a blanket, and spread it out. Mom got out some sandwiches, fruit, and crackers. James and Morgan took out the juice. The Parkers sprawled out on Andrews Bald and ate while enjoying the hazy views.

SHORT ON TOP

There are several high-elevation balds in the Great Smoky Mountains. Andrews Bald is one of the best known. Historically, farmers would drive their livestock to the highest balds in the summer. Grazing cattle would keep many of these areas free of trees. Today, the park service maintains the balds by cutting back the new growth.

James took a bite of his peanut butter and jelly sandwich. "Good idea, Mom," he said with his mouth half full.

The sun disappeared behind a cloud. A flickering of light was followed several seconds later by a low, persistent drumroll of thunder.

"It sounds like the sky's stomach is growling again," Morgan said.

Mom pulled out the parkas just as the first drops of rain plunked down. "Always be prepared," she said.

They quickly packed up their picnic and headed for the forest just as the storm broke loose.

Rain pelted down on the trail, which quickly resembled a trickling stream. The Parkers hustled along and caught up to a man carrying an insect net. The man plodded along slowly, unfazed by the weather.

"Excuse us," Mom said as she led her family by.

James passed the man last and asked, "What are you trying to catch?"

Morgan, Mom, and Dad stopped and listened for the answer.

"I work for the National Park Service," the man replied. "We're out here studying certain types of flies. But right now volunteers all over the park are doing what is called a bio-blitz. Naturalists are working around the clock to identify as many living things as possible, and we're sure finding a lot, even some insects we didn't know existed."

"We saw some pretty unusual moths at our campground bathroom," Morgan informed him.

"Ah, yes, moths and butterflies," the man mused. "We are very interested in those too, and we've recently discovered at least fifty new species here! We now know that there are over 1,600 species of moths and butterflies that live in the Smokies."

"Did you see that black-and-red-striped beetle back there on the trail?" James asked.

"Beetles, the most common of all insects," the man replied. "There are over 250,000 beetle species in the world, and the Smokies has over 2,500 types. I didn't see the beetle you were talking about, though. I wish I had.

"This whole place is an entomologist's gold mine," the man continued. "We think there might be over 100,000 total forms of life in the park. That may be the most in one place on the planet."

Lightning flickered and thunder rumbled again. The Parkers said good-bye to the bug catcher and hustled up the trail. They arrived at the parking lot just as the storm eased up. Morgan, James, Mom, and Dad looked at the steamy, wet asphalt walkway leading up to Clingmans Dome.

Dad checked his watch and the brightening sky. "It's noon," he announced. "Shall we?"

Morgan, James, Mom, and Dad walked quickly up the trail. The sun was peeking through where they were, but clouds and fog still clung tightly to the summit ahead.

Soon they approached a circular, raised cement walkway leading to a round tower. The family wound their way toward the top.

"It looks like we're heading into a UFO," Morgan joked.

"Or a ride at Disneyland," Mom added.

The Parkers stepped onto the tower at Clingmans Dome. Signs posted along the viewing platform pointed out mountains in the distance. But all the family could see were clouds being whipped across the horizon.

"I guess we're *supposed* to see out there," James commented.

"What we can see up close, though, is interesting enough," Mom said. "Look at all those dead trees."

"It looks like a ghost forest," Dad said.

"Why are the trees all dying?" Morgan asked.

"I heard," Mom replied, "that an insect called the balsam woolly adelgid is killing them. Also, acid rain and pollution are adding to the problem."

ACID RAIN

Rainfall in the Great Smoky Mountains is five to ten times more acidic than normal rainwater. This can harm the park's plants and animals. Clouds hanging over the spruce-fir forests around Clingmans Dome, the highest peak in the Great Smoky Mountains, can be as acidic as vinegar. Acid rain can also fall out of the atmosphere as a dry deposit of tiny particles. Coal-burning power plants and emissions from cars in large cities nearby are the main causes of acid rain in the park.

Dad looked at the large raindrops beginning to plunk onto the dying forest. "We should get off this peak now."

Morgan, James, Mom, and Dad jogged the half mile down to the parking lot. The shuttle was waiting when they arrived.

The driver rolled down her window. "Hop in!" she called out. The Parkers piled into van, and the driver took off to Newfound Gap.

"It's not even raining down here," James noticed.

The driver smiled. "Oh, I'm sure it will be, real soon."

A few minutes later, the Parkers arrived at Newfound Gap.

Morgan, James, Mom, and Dad piled out of the shuttle and grabbed their backpacks.

"Three days of backpacking to our car waiting at Cosby," James announced.

"Can you deliver a pizza out to the Icewater Spring shelter tonight?" Dad joked.

The driver smiled and then pointed to the clouds. "You better get going," she suggested.

First the family wandered over to a large stone memorial.

"It's a statue of Franklin Delano Roosevelt," Morgan realized. She looked at the sign with the picture of the former president giving his dedication speech. Morgan closed her eyes and imagined herself there, standing next to her great-grandfather, who wore CCC work clothes.

Dad cleared his throat and began reading from the information plaque in a bold, presidential voice. "We meet today to dedicate the mountains, streams, and forests to the service of the American people…"

Morgan opened her eyes. "You sounded very dignified," she complimented him.

Dad stood up tall. "Maybe it's time for me to make a run for office."

Then Dad laughed. "Or not!"

Finally the Parkers walked over to the trail. Morgan took several pictures of her family at the mileage sign.

"The Appalachian Trail at last," Dad announced. "At least a small part of it."

"How long is the whole thing?" James asked.

"Over 2,100 miles," Dad answered. "And it goes through fourteen states, from Georgia all the way to Maine."

Morgan stopped and looked at her father. "Fourteen states?"

"Yep," Dad answered. "But don't think our short trek is going to be easy. The trail through the Smokies is supposed to be rough and remote."

The Parkers began their journey. "What are those white marks on the trees for?" Morgan asked.

"I think," Dad replied, "those marks show we're on the AT Trail."

"You mean they have them all the way to Maine?" James asked.

"All the way," Dad said. "Consider them our escorts."

"As well as these delicate bouquets of bluish lavender flowers," Mom added. "They seem to be lining our path."

Mom pulled a laminated wildflower sheet out of her pack. She studied it for a minute while glancing at the flowers. "I think they're thyme-leaved bluets," Mom announced. "They bloom in June in the high elevations of the park."

The trail followed the ridge of the mountains with views into deep wooded valleys far below.

"At least we don't have to carry our tents," James said.

The Parkers got into the rhythm of the hike. The high alpine forest was full of ferns, mosses, and dense underbrush. Clouds drifted by and engulfed the forest as they traveled.

At 1.7 miles they reached the junction to the Kephart Trail. Morgan slipped off her backpack. "Can I rest a minute?" she asked. She put her pack against a tree and plopped down on a rock. Morgan wiped some sweat off her forehead, then scratched the back of her head and neck. *I'm still itchy from that tick*, she thought. Then she remembered their picnic in the grass at Andrews Bald a few hours ago. Morgan quickly stood up. *That's weird. My legs and back are sore*, she realized.

Dark clouds continued to drift about. At times it seemed late in the day, but then the sun would poke through and the forest would quickly brighten up.

Mom passed James some trail mix. He grabbed a handful then passed the bag to Morgan.

"No, thanks," Morgan replied while scratching under her arm.

Thunder rumbled in the distance.

"Come on," Dad called out. "I think our shelter is calling us."

Morgan, James, Mom, and Dad put their parkas back on. They hustled along as rain began to plunk down. Their feet squished along the wet, soggy trail.

Soon they passed the Boulevard Trail junction.

A short while later they came to a shelter just off the trail. It was in an open area, clear of trees. "It's like a miniature bald here," Mom said.

The Parkers hurried out of the rain and into the three-sided structure. They placed their packs against two large wooden shelves near the back. "Welcome to Icewater Spring shelter, our home for the night," Dad announced.

Morgan, James, Mom, and Dad started unpacking. "Where do we sleep?" James asked.

Mom looked around. She gestured to the two wooden shelves. "On those, I'm sure."

"Really?" Morgan asked.

"Don't worry," Dad said. "With our mattress pads, camping pillows, and sleeping bags, we'll have all the comforts of home. And," Dad said, pointing to a bench with a thin wooden slab above it, "we can cook over here and still stay dry out of the rain."

The Parkers set up for their night at the shelter.

Mom strung up a clothesline. "That way, even if it's raining, at least we'll start tomorrow in dry clothes," she explained.

Meanwhile, Morgan and James blew up the air mattresses and placed them side by side on the lower wooden slot. They fluffed up their sleeping bags and pillows and spread them out on top of the mattresses.

Dad boiled a pot of water on the wooden board above the bench. He added several bags of ramen noodles, then mixed in some dried vegetables and tofu.

Morgan, James, and Mom joined Dad. The four of them sat down and watched the rain drip while their pot of soup cooked.

James looked at the gear spread out in their corner of the sleeping area. "I wonder if we're going to be the only ones here tonight."

"Well, there's supposedly room for twelve," Mom said. "But maybe the weather will keep a few people away. Either way, we'll make it work."

Dad lifted up some ramen with his fork and tasted it. "It's ready," he announced, then dished the soup into their plastic bowls.

James took a sip of the hot, savory dinner. "It's perfect."

"I agree," Mom acknowledged. "But I think we're biased toward the cook."

"Biased toward the cook?" James inquired.

Mom smiled. "It means that since we like Dad, we're naturally going to prefer his cooking."

Mom passed around some crackers to go with the soup. Afterward, James found the bag of chocolate chip cookies for dessert.

They passed the cookies back and forth while staring at the wet forest. Morgan didn't take any.

Rain continued to drip down, but it had eased up a bit. In the distant sky a brief burst of sunlight illuminated the horizon.

Other hikers had now made it to the shelter. They, too, had set up their gear, hung up clothes to dry, and were preparing dinner.

Morgan looked back at all the camping gear strewn about. She counted the sleeping bags. "It looks like there are ten people staying here tonight."

Dad noticed how dark it was becoming. "Let's get everything cleaned up and put away now, okay?"

"And then," Mom added, "once we're all tucked in, I've got another journal entry to read."

Dad cleaned the dishes and put away the stove. Mom joined James and Morgan to filter water. Meanwhile, Dad took all the food and scented items and placed them in their stuff sacks. He walked over to the bear cables and clipped the sacks in. Then Dad hoisted the stuff sacks high up off the ground.

Dad walked back to the shelter. Morgan, James, and Mom were already snug in their sleeping bags, each wearing a headlamp.

Then Dad slithered into his own bag. Once he was comfortable, Mom opened the journal to a marked page and read.

July 27, 1939

Max Davis here.

It's the summer of 1939. I'm spending another season in the wilderness building trails in the park.

Our base camp is NP-5, or "Camp Kephart Prong." It isn't a bad place to be, but sometimes we're lucky enough to get shipped over to Cades Cove.

Yesterday we had one of those days. The fellas and I played some softball. Afterward, we got in some billiards, but I lost to Freckles. At the end of the day I checked out a few books at the library, took in a show at the minstrel house, and even got a rare hot shower (it had been a few weeks!).

But now we're back clearing a trail right out of the mountain high above where we're camped.

"Wait a minute!" James whispered. He sat up and reached for his pack. James pulled out his park map and unfolded it. "We passed Kephart junction today." James shone his headlamp on the map.

"There's Kephart Camp!" Morgan said.

"So somewhere down there, my grandfather camped with the CCC," Mom realized.

"That means," Dad added, "that the section of trail we're on just might be the part he cleared."

The Parkers heard a few people turning over in their sleeping bags. Morgan looked outside. It was now pitch black.

"Maybe I should put the journal away for now," Mom said.

James lay back down. "Can't you just finish this page?"

Mom looked around at the dark shelter full of hikers trying to sleep. "I'd better not," she whispered.

Morgan, James, Mom, and Dad turned out their lights and slid deeper into their sleeping bags. Somewhere on the other end of the room, a person was snoring lightly. James looked at Morgan and grinned, but she couldn't see him in the dark.

Drips of rain pattered down on the metal roof. Tiny scratching sounds came from somewhere. And now, several people were snoring.

Eventually, each of the Parkers drifted off to sleep.

At some point, James felt something tickle the top of his feet. Then, a small, scratchy feeling crept up his legs. *Is there something alive in my bag?* he wondered.

James lay still. He listened to Morgan next to him. Her breathing told James she was sleeping.

Suddenly, James felt something tiny hop off his sleeping bag and land on his chest. James carefully reached back and grabbed his headlamp. He turned it on and held it up.

A tiny mouse was staring right at him. "Ahh!" James shrieked while swatting at the mouse.

The rodent dashed back the way it came. James shook his whole body and bumped into Morgan, who rolled into Mom and Dad. Now all four Parkers were awake.

Dad looked over at James. "What happened?"

"A mouse was on me!" James exclaimed.

"Where is it now?" Mom asked.

"It ran away," James answered.

Mom searched with her headlamp, but she couldn't find the mouse.

James scrunched deeper into his sleeping bag. It took a while, but eventually James went back to sleep.

Sometime later, Morgan woke up. She tried to concentrate on any sounds a mouse might make while scratching its way through holes in the wood. But nothing sounded like a mouse. Morgan did hear her own heavy breathing. *Do I have asthma?* she worried.

Morgan rolled onto her stomach and noticed how achy her body felt. She peered outside through the opening at the front of the shelter. It was still pitch black, clammy, and wet outside. But Morgan couldn't tell if it was raining or not.

Morgan felt something itchy near her neck and shoulders.

She scratched herself. *I bet I look like a cat itching a flea,* she thought.

But the itching didn't go away. Morgan scratched harder. "Get off me!" she gasped.

Mom rolled over and flicked on her headlamp.

"I think there's another tick on me," Morgan whispered.

"Lean your head over here," Mom directed her.

Mom shone the light on Morgan and sifted through her hair. But she couldn't see anything.

"Is everything okay?" Dad asked.

"No!" Morgan called out.

Several people in the shelter shifted around in their sleeping bags.

"Let's walk outside so we don't bother anyone," Mom said.

Mom put on her headlamp and grabbed her day pack. Morgan and Mom slipped into their shoes and jackets and walked away from the shelter. The rain had stopped, but everything was muddy and wet. Morgan looked up but couldn't see any stars.

"Turn around," Mom directed Morgan.

Mom carefully checked through Morgan's hair. "Aha!" she declared.

"What?"

"You've got another tick back here."

"I thought so," Morgan gulped.

"Hold still, honey," Mom said.

"Why me?" Morgan asked. She thought again about the picnic at Andrews Bald. "Do you think it's because we were lying down in the grass?"

"It might have gotten caught in your long hair," Mom replied. "But the rest of us could have ticks too. We'll have to do another complete tick check in the morning."

Mom brushed Morgan's hair aside. "Oh, no," she said.

"What?"

"It's engorged," Mom replied.

"What's that mean?" Morgan asked nervously.

"It means," Mom explained, "it's been feeding on you. And it's filled with your blood."

"Yuck!" Morgan shuddered nervously. "Can you get it off me? Fast?"

"I have to do it carefully," Mom replied. "Otherwise it can get stuck inside you. And get you sick."

I wonder if I'm sick already, Morgan thought.

Mom reached over to her day pack. She pulled out the first-aid kit and fished through it. "I knew these would come in handy someday," she said, holding out a pair of tweezers. "Hold still, Morgan."

Morgan grimaced as Mom, like a surgeon, slowly moved the tweezers closer to the tick. "Okay, here goes."

Morgan looked at the ground. "It's like I'm having an operation," she observed.

Mom placed the tweezers around the tick's head. She gently but firmly pulled the tick out. "Got it!"

Morgan looked at Mom. "So it's all gone?"

"All gone," Mom confirmed.

Mom used a bacterial pad to clean off Morgan's tick bite. By then dawn was breaking and rays of sun were poking above the horizon to the east. "Well at least the day's going to start out sunny," Mom said.

Morgan and Mom walked back into the shelter. James and Dad were lying there awake. "Where have you been?" James asked.

"Mom had to operate and get a tick out of me," Morgan answered.

The Parkers walked off into the woods.

Dad and James went in one direction and Morgan and Mom in the other. They worked in pairs to check for ticks on each other. They put on clean clothes and wrapped their dirty ones in garbage bags, then met back at the shelter.

"We didn't find any others right now," Mom reported. "But we should check again later."

"We should also tuck our pant legs into our socks and wear long sleeves," Dad added. "That way our skin is almost all covered."

"And I'm putting my hair in a ponytail," Morgan chimed in.

The Parkers ate breakfast and finished packing.

Morgan took a picture of her family posed in front of the shelter before they took off on the trail.

The path, like on the day before, followed a ridgeline with steep drop-offs in both directions. Dad gazed down at a valley far below. "And I always thought the Appalachian Mountains weren't rugged," he said. "Now I know that's not true."

The Parkers trekked on. The sun was shining, and it was pleasantly cool and dry.

Morgan's leg muscles felt funny. She stopped

hiking and shook her legs out. Then Morgan leaned over and tried to calm her breathing. Dad came up to her. "Are you okay?" he asked.

"I think so," Morgan lied.

At a bend in the trail, Mom stopped. She gazed out at a large bulge of rock jutting out above the ridge. James, Dad, and Morgan joined Mom.

"Charlies Bunion!" Dad exclaimed.

The Parkers approached the rock formation. A warning sign said CHARLIES BUNION—CLOSELY CONTROL CHILDREN. A side trail led right to it.

"Let's stay together," Mom said.

The whole area near the trail became more and more rocky. And the plants and trees were stunted, sheared by the wind. "It kind of looks like a Japanese bonsai garden around here," Mom described. "Everything is in miniature."

Near the end of the rock outcropping, the family put down their packs, climbed up a small, protruding point, and stood up. "Look at the clouds being whipped across the peaks," Dad exclaimed.

"Yeah, it's windy up here too," Mom added. "Let's get back to the trail."

The Parkers climbed back down. Dad pulled out some trail mix. "Snack time," he announced.

Mom grabbed a handful and passed the bag to James. James took some trail mix and handed it to Morgan. "No, thanks," Morgan said.

James looked at Morgan, thinking, *That's not like her.*

The Parkers spent a few more minutes at Charlies Bunion. Then they packed up and continued on their journey.

Morgan, James, Mom, and Dad rejoined the AT Trail after the short side trail to the bunion. Again the family hiked along following the rolling ridgeline.

James caught a glimpse of an orange centipede crawling slowly along the path. He bent down to inspect it.

Mom caught up to James. "Pretty, isn't it?" she said.

The Parkers hiked on in silence, except for the sounds of their footsteps crunching and unseen birds chirping and singing in the forest.

The trail continued to roll along, and as it did, the family gradually spread out. Soon Morgan was behind her parents, who trailed James.

They approached a crew of young men and women strewn along a short section of trail. Morgan noticed picks, shovels, and wheelbarrows scattered among the trail crew. They were busy clearing the trail but paused briefly to let the Parkers pass.

"Hey, this is what your grandfather did," James said to Mom.

"Yep," Mom said. "It's good to know that groups like the CCC are still maintaining the AT Trail today."

After passing the crew, Dad stopped for a second and wiped sweat off his forehead. "This is a hard trail!" he muttered.

"Hard trail" echoed in Morgan's head. *It does feel extra hard*, she realized. *Or is something wrong with me?* Morgan's back and legs ached even more. *I feel like I've been hiking forever*, she thought. Then Morgan looked up, and the scene she saw was very different.

The Smokies in Morgan's mind were now in black and white. Morgan imagined the trail builders of the past coming to life.

Everyone her great-grandfather had written about was there: Freckles, Mop Head, Slim, and Jar Head.

Morgan walked by the imaginary trail crew toiling away at the difficult work. Some were using shovels to haul away chunks of dirt and small rocks. Others pounded axes into the ground, breaking down the rock into smaller pieces, then tossing the rocks into the woods. And some were hammering in wooden planks along the trail. The crew seemed oblivious as Morgan walked by. One crew member glanced at Morgan, then scratched under his arm.

Morgan trudged along looking for a familiar face. Finally, a tall, slender man stood up and leaned over on his axe. He was coated in dirt and sweat and nodded to Morgan. Now I know why they call him Bean Pole, *Morgan realized.*

Morgan approached the man. She grabbed her water bottle and held it out to her parched great-grandfather. "Thanks," *he replied, then took a long gulp.* "I needed a break. This hard work is really taking its toll on me."

Dad put his hand on Morgan's shoulder. She finished drinking water from her bottle, then looked up at her dad.

"Are you okay?" he asked.

"Yes," Morgan replied.

"I turned a corner on the trail and looked back for a second and didn't see you," Dad explained. "Boy, did that make my heart jump. So I ran back to get you."

"Thanks," Morgan said. "I guess I was daydreaming. And I stopped to drink some water. Where's Mom and James?"

"They're waiting up ahead."

Morgan and Dad rejoined James and Mom and they all continued hiking.

The trail seemed to go on and on. Morgan struggled to keep up. Each hill seemed to be more of a burden. Morgan soon fell behind again.

This time, Mom stopped to wait for her.

"Sorry," Morgan said when she caught up.

"There's no need to say you're sorry," Mom replied. "I saw you back there, so I stopped."

The late afternoon sun filtered through the trees. Morgan, James, Mom, and Dad all walked slowly. "I think we're running out of gas," Dad said seriously.

Finally, after what seemed like endless hiking, James saw a trail junction sign. "Pecks Corner!" he exclaimed.

James waited at the junction for the rest of his family to arrive. Morgan took off her pack and gingerly sat down. "Can't we just camp here?"

James looked at the sign. "The shelter's just four-tenths of a mile down this trail."

"Let's just hang out for a few minutes," Mom suggested.

A while later, Morgan slowly stood up. "Okay, I think I'm ready now."

The Parkers headed to Pecks Corner.

Soon enough, they passed the privy and bear wires and arrived at the wooden shelter.

Morgan grabbed her mattress pad and unrolled it, placing it on the lower wooden shelf. She put her pillow down and crawled onto the pad without even blowing it up.

Dad came over and fluffed out Morgan's sleeping bag. He put it on top of her. "How are you?" he asked.

Morgan looked up, glassy-eyed. "I feel awful," she finally admitted.

Dad unrolled his mattress pad and blew it up.

He put it down next to Morgan. "Here, roll over onto this, it'll feel better."

Morgan followed Dad's suggestion. "It hurts to move," she complained.

Dad moved the sleeping bag back on top of Morgan. "Is anything else bothering you?" he asked.

"My stomach hurts, and I'm dizzy like I have the flu. I feel like I'm going to throw up."

Dad felt Morgan's head. "Just a second, I'll be right back."

Dad walked over to Mom, who was helping James prepare dinner. "Where's the first-aid kit?" he inquired.

Mom nodded toward the side. "It's in our stuff sacks."

Dad went to the supplies and fished around until he found the kit. He opened it and pulled out the thermometer. Then he returned to Morgan.

Morgan stared up at Dad. Her face was flushed and sweaty.

Dad placed the thermometer under Morgan's tongue, and Morgan held it in place.

Dad looked at Morgan, then at his watch. He stared off into the woods and waited. "We'll make you some soup," Dad said. Then, after a few minutes, he took the thermometer from her mouth and glanced at it.

"Is it bad?" Morgan asked.

"No," Dad answered. "You don't have a fever. But obviously something's wrong."

Mom came over. "How long have you been feeling sick?" she asked.

Morgan closed her eyes and tried to remember. "The last couple of days, really," she answered. "It's just gotten a lot worse today."

Mom gently combed her fingers through Morgan's hair. "Why didn't you tell us?"

"I didn't want to ruin the backpack," Morgan replied.

"Sweetheart, your health is a lot more important than this backpack," Mom said. Then Mom and Dad stepped away and started talking.

Morgan rolled over and saw James stirring something on the stove. Then she looked around the room.

Pecks Corner was now crowded with people. Backpacks, mattresses, and sleeping bags were strewn about. Morgan slowly sat up. She saw that the upper bunk was full of camping gear too. And several other hikers were also cooking dinner just a short distance away.

Morgan slowly lay back down. Then she heard Dad's voice. "A ranger!" he said. Dad walked over to the person in uniform.

Morgan listened to their conversation.

"Actually, I'm a Ridge Runner," the woman replied.

"Well, you're just the person we're looking for," Dad said. Then he gestured toward Morgan. "Our daughter's sick."

Morgan saw Dad and the Ridge Runner talking earnestly. Mom came over to join them. Meanwhile, James turned off the stove, covered the pasta, and stepped away from the shelter to drain the water. James ducked down as drops of water kept falling on him. *It's raining again,* Morgan realized. Then Morgan saw James return to refill the pot and start boiling water for soup.

Meanwhile, Mom, Dad, and the Ridge Runner walked over to Morgan.

The Ridge Runner smiled at Morgan. "This isn't a great place to get sick, is it?"

Morgan shook her head.

"There's one thing we can check now," the Ridge Runner said. "Can you look at where you removed the tick and see if there's a red, circular mark around the bite? It would appear like a bull's-eye."

Since it was nearly dark, Mom pulled out a flashlight. Morgan propped herself up. Mom shone the light back and forth on Morgan's head and neck. "I don't see anything like a round bull's-eye," Mom reported. "There is a red mark, though."

"Hmm." The Ridge Runner thought. "You did say the tick was embedded in there. The red mark might be swelling or an infection. Have you cleaned the area out?"

"Absolutely," Mom responded.

Dad looked at the Ridge Runner anxiously. "Are tick bites problematic here?"

"Ticks can transmit diseases from their bites," the Ridge Runner explained. "It's very rare. Still, Lyme disease and Rocky Mountain spotted fever are quite serious. If that's what she has, it's best to get her to a doctor as soon as possible."

Morgan looked at her dad, then at the Ridge Runner. "Are you going to have to rescue me out of here in a helicopter?"

"We'll carry you out of here ourselves first before we even think about that," Dad responded.

The Ridge Runner chimed in. "There are several rescue and medical alternatives available," she said. "But there's also the chance she has something else."

Mom came over to Morgan with a cup of warm soup. "Can you try drinking some?" she asked.

Morgan sat straight up. "I'm really nauseous," she groaned.

"I think getting at least a little warm food in you might help," Mom said.

Morgan slid down to the wooden step below her sleeping area. She took the warm soup and managed a small sip.

Mom smiled at Morgan, then looked at the Ridge Runner. "Since we're not certain what's wrong, why don't we wait and see how she's doing in the morning?"

"Okay," the Ridge Runner agreed. "And I have my radio if we need it." She walked off and chatted with the other hikers.

Morgan slowly drank some more soup. Then she leaned back. It was nearly dark, and the other trekkers were cleaning up and getting ready for bed.

Rain poured steadily down outside and cascaded off the roof, showering the perimeter of the shelter. The inside, although dry from the rain, was musty, cool, and damp. By the light of the lantern, Morgan noticed steam pouring from her mouth as she breathed.

Dad and James came in with rainwater dripping off their parkas. They hung up their wet gear. "We've got fresh water," Dad announced. "And all the food is hung up in our stuff sacks."

James walked up to his sister and sat next to her. "How are you?"

"I wish I was home in bed," she answered. Then she shivered. "I want to get back in my sleeping bag."

The Parkers organized the rest of their gear and piled into their nook in Pecks Corner. Mom and Dad slept toward the middle, followed by Morgan. James was up against the wall. Eight other people also stayed in the shelter, two more on the bottom rack and six on top.

Morgan could hear people shifting around in their sleeping bags. Her stomach growled angrily, and she felt a wave of wooziness sweep through her body. Morgan grabbed her stomach.

"I have to go to the bathroom," Morgan whispered to Mom.

Mom turned over. "Now?"

"Yes," Morgan answered urgently.

Morgan and Mom got out of bed. They turned on their headlamps and put on their rain gear. Mom put her arm around Morgan and guided her into the woods, heading for the privy.

As they hurried along the rainy, wet path, Morgan remembered how going to the bathroom was for the Walker sisters. In the distance she and Mom saw the privy at the top of a small hill. Mom guided Morgan to the door and unlatched it. Morgan lunged inside, lifted the lid of the toilet, and threw up.

Later, back in bed, Morgan kept her eyes closed, hoping that would help her sleep. She saw light flickering through her closed eyelids. Then, somewhere in the distance, thunder rumbled. The rain poured down even harder. It cascaded off the roof in buckets, and Morgan could hear trees rustling in the wind.

Morgan rolled over and opened her eyes. She looked outside through the opening of the shelter and waited.

The sky lit up brightly and flickered off and on for a second or two. Morgan got a brief glimpse of the colorless, ghostlike world that surrounded her before everything quickly became dark again. Then, thunder boomed loudly. Morgan scrunched into her sleeping bag.

Lightning flashed again. This time, Morgan saw a tiny mouse scampering across the dirt floor of the shelter. Then, deafening thunder chased her deeper into her bag and up against Mom. *It's going to be a long night,* Morgan thought.

Finally, exhaustion got the best of Morgan. She drifted into a restless sleep.

Morgan was now wrapped in a blanket, sitting on the porch of an old wooden cabin. Several women were going about their business. One was peeling apples and dropping them into a bucket, another was spinning yarn using her spinning wheel. One was off to the side, writing in a journal. Another sister was peeling potatoes.

One of the women came over with an antique-looking saucer. The liquid in it steamed up into the cool, damp air. "This tea always helps us when we're sick," the woman said.

Morgan took a sip of the soothing, warm drink. Then she noticed several centipedes on the floor of the cabin. One started crawling up the blanket Morgan was wrapped in. Trapped, Morgan watched the large insect climb higher. Then, to Morgan's horror, she noticed a frenzy of ticks were also on the blanket. Morgan looked at all the ticks scurrying about. She tossed and turned, hoping to throw them off.

But the ticks did something unusual: They shed their shells and transformed into a flurry of moths and butterflies. The winged creatures immediately took flight. They fluttered about looking for a place to land in a beautiful garden full of fruit trees and flowers, which had replaced the cabin. Morgan ran around the garden delightfully. The moths and butterflies followed her, some landing on Morgan's arms and head. Morgan twirled around, enjoying the bright, warm sunshine. She headed for the open, grassy bald at the top of the mountain. But then Morgan tripped on a rock and fell into a slick, muddy ravine. Morgan scrambled back to her feet and realized she was in the middle of a cemetery in a driving rainstorm. The graveyard was filled with tombstones from early

pioneers. Morgan noticed an engraving on a tomb: 1894–1904, Sarah lived barely ten years. Morgan gulped in her sleep. That's my age, *she realized.*

Morgan saw several of the moths and butterflies still fluttering about. What the butterflies didn't see was that the tombs all around her were infested with salamanders. Some of the salamanders were tiny, but several were well over a foot in length. A few of the salamanders clutched nets between their toes. They held their nets up, trying to catch an unsuspecting moth or butterfly. Still the winged insects hovered closer, looking for a place to land.

Suddenly, Morgan felt compelled to warn the butterflies and moths of their impending doom.

"No!" Morgan shouted. Then she turned around and noticed several other butterflies approaching the ground.

The salamanders, some crawling on the gravestones, lifted their eyes, opened their mouths, and salivated, anticipating their imminent meal.

"No!" Morgan shouted. "Don't land! It's not time to die!"

Morgan bolted upward. She shot out of her dream and was instantly awake. Morgan noticed that dawn was breaking and light was creeping into the shelter.

Morgan looked around frantically. She wondered if she had yelled out loud and woken anyone. But everyone appeared to still be asleep. Morgan scratched her arm. She kept scratching, then noticed James's eyes were open. They looked at each other. "You were having a bad dream, weren't you?" James asked.

"Did I say anything?" Morgan asked.

"No," James lied. "Are you feeling better?"

"I'm itchy," Morgan replied, then scratched some more.

Morgan looked up. Her parents were talking to the Ridge Runner again. The Ridge Runner had a park service radio in her hands. "What are they talking about?" she asked James.

"You."

"We could get medical personnel up here," the Ridge Runner said, "to assess her condition. But I can also call in and get advice."

"If it is from ticks," Mom asked, "it's very serious, right?"

"The onset of a tickborne illness is three to fourteen days or longer," the Ridge Runner explained. "That tick was on Morgan just two days ago."

"Unless she had one on her earlier that we didn't know about," Mom added.

Mom, Dad, and the Ridge Runner talked some more. Then Dad spoke emphatically, "Wait, hold on. Let's see how Morgan is doing first."

Morgan looked at her parents. "Something's on me again!" she yelled.

Morgan got up and put on her shoes. She wobbled toward Mom, Dad, and the Ridge Runner.

Mom took Morgan's hand. "Let me take a look."

They walked to a private place outside the shelter. "Where is it?" Mom inquired.

Morgan lifted her arm. "In here."

Mom took a closer look. "Yep!" she exclaimed.

"It's another one, right?" Morgan asked nervously.

"I'm afraid so."

Mom dashed back to the shelter and grabbed her first-aid kit. Then she carefully removed the swollen tick from Morgan. They walked back and joined the others.

"Did you get it?" the Ridge Runner asked.

"Yes," Mom replied.

"Okay," the Ridge Runner said. "Let me know how you would like me to proceed."

The Parkers hung out for a while and ate breakfast. Morgan had a packet of oatmeal. "I'm actually a little hungry," she realized.

After breakfast, Morgan put on her backpack.

"What are you doing?" Mom asked.

"I want to see if I can carry this while hiking."

Morgan walked back and forth in the shelter with the pack on. "I don't feel 100 percent," Morgan announced, "but I think I can hike."

Dad looked at Morgan. "Okay," he agreed. Then he glanced at the Ridge Runner.

"I'll alert the trail patrol at Tricorner Knob to check on you," the Ridge Runner said. "She'll also be able to get a medic up there if necessary."

"Sounds like a plan," Dad responded.

Mom stuffed Morgan's sleeping bag into her own pack and handed the air mattress to Dad. James took one of Morgan's water bottles.

Dad put his arm around Morgan. "Personally, I don't know if I'd be hiking today if I were in your shoes. I think you're rather remarkable."

Morgan smiled. "Well, let's go then!"

The Parkers hit the trail at 10:00 a.m. The air was fresh and cool after the rain, and the sky was a powder blue.

They hiked on, skirting the summit of Mount Sequoyah. James walked next to Morgan and watched for insects and salamanders along the trail.

Soon they came to a small rock outcropping.

James looked at a metal circle embedded in the rock. *5,849 feet* was inscribed on it. "Is that our elevation?"

"That's right," Dad answered. "And if I remember correctly, this is the high mark on the trail today, as well as the halfway point."

Dad looked at Morgan and James and Mom. "Let's rest and have some lunch here, okay?"

Mom and Dad started pulling out food. "Can I have one of those apples?" Morgan asked.

After eating, Morgan stood up. She slowly put on her backpack, then addressed her family. "I think I can take on more weight now."

"It's okay, all our packs are getting lighter with the food we've eaten," Mom answered. "How do you feel?"

"Better," Morgan answered. "What do you think I had?"

"I'm not sure," Dad answered. "Maybe the flu. But whatever it was, it seems to be going away."

The Parkers continued trudging along.

Just before the Balsam Mountain junction, a short side path led to the Tricorner Knob shelter.

Morgan, James, Mom, and Dad took the trail. Tricorner Knob shelter was a bit more modern looking than the other shelters where they'd stayed. It had a fire ring and a tarp that could be rolled down to keep out the weather. A water pipe and the privy were nearby.

The Parkers set up, again putting their gear in the lower right-hand corner of the sleeping area.

After dinner, Morgan, James, Mom, and Dad played some cards. They watched the sky slowly darken over the quiet forest.

Mom and Dad cleaned up while Morgan got into bed. James pulled out his journal.

> This is James Parker reporting.
>
> Morgan is getting better now. What a relief. We didn't know what we were going to have to do to get her out of here.
>
> By the time we get back to our car tomorrow we'll have completed a twenty-six-mile backpack. Most of it will be on the Appalachian Trail. But there's so much more of this trail to hike on. I can't believe it goes all the way from Georgia to Maine. Dad says it takes about five to six <u>months</u> to do. Morgan and I are already talking about covering the whole trail sometime. Maybe when we're in college.
>
> But at the same time, as Mom says, "There's so much to see in such a short distance." More than anything else, I think Mom means the bugs and insects. She studied botany in college. But after visiting here, she keeps talking about entomology. And I can see why, with the stuff we're seeing. I love those macaroni-and-cheese-colored centipedes!
>
> Anyway, it's nearly dark now and everyone's piling into bed. So I better join them...
>
> Reporting from the Smokies,
> James Parker

James put his journal away and got into his sleeping bag. He propped his head up and looked outside. The last bit of evening light silhouetted the forest. Then, slowly, all became dark.

"Goodnight, everyone," Dad said.

"Goodnight," Morgan replied.

Early the next morning, the Parkers woke to clear skies.

Dad looked at Morgan, who was sleeping next to Mom and James, then he got up out of his sleeping bag and prepared breakfast.

A few minutes later, Morgan joined him. "How are you doing, sunshine?" he asked.

Morgan looked at the shelter and at the morning sunlight filtering through the trees. "Much better," she reported. "A couple of days ago, I wanted nothing else but to be back home in bed. Now I wish we had more time to see the park."

"That's great to hear," Dad replied. "I'm completely relieved."

"Me too," Morgan added.

The first part of the day the trail skirted up the flank of Mount Guyot. Morgan, James, Mom, and Dad were back in the high country of the Smokies.

Mom noticed the trees. "We're surrounded by a subalpine forest again," she reported. "I wonder what the elevation is here."

"We're going to have to get an altimeter to carry with us on our hikes," Dad said. "But I bet close to 6,000 feet."

Once they passed Mount Guyot, the trail began a long, steady descent. James noticed that far below, tiny-looking clearings and homes lay beyond the park border. "They're way down there," he commented.

"It's nice to see signs of civilization," Mom added. "But I'm going to miss camping in the wilderness."

A while later, the Parkers met up with the Snake Den Ridge Trail junction and took it. They walked farther and farther down. "I'm glad we're not going up this," Morgan said.

James looked at the trees surrounding the trail. "Hey, there aren't any more white stripes. They must only mark the AT Trail."

The rocky, wet trail was more treacherous than hiking along the ridge. Morgan, James, Mom, and Dad carefully walked down the steep path.

The trail continued zigzagging briskly down. Morgan stopped and pulled out her camera. "Look at this weird fungus on the tree!" The unusual growth was golden yellow and white.

James came over to look. "I think it sort of looks like a scrambled egg," he said.

Then they approached a grove of rhododendron in full bloom. "There are some more of our purple flowers," Mom announced.

Later, the Parkers stopped and admired some shrubs with bright orange flowers. "Flaming azalea," Mom said. "You know, this whole park is like a garden nursery."

They continued on. Soon, the forest became dark and dense again. "We're back in the lowlands," Mom acknowledged.

The trail was now accompanied by the sound of water.

"Salamanders!" James called out.

The Parkers came to a boulder-strewn stream crossing. "This is a good place to filter up and have some snacks," Dad suggested.

James was the first one to haul off his pack. Then he hopped over to the gurgling stream. "Hey, salamanders, where are you?" he whispered.

Fraser fir

American
beech

Tulip
tree

Hemlock

Mountain
laurel

There are five distinct forest types in the Smokies. The type of forest in each area is determined by elevation, moisture, soil type, and amount of sun hitting the slope.

Spruce-Fir Forest: The most easily identified forest type in the Smokies. Evergreen trees of Fraser fir and red spruce are typically on the highest peaks, above 4,500 feet. Often called the Canadian zone because this type of forest is usually found in Canada.

Northern Hardwood Forest: Dominated by American beech and yellow birch trees. This forest type is referred to as North Woods because forests like this are often found in New England and the Great Lakes. Elevations of this forest are 4,500 to 6,000 feet.

Cove Hardwood: The most diverse forest in the Smokies. If the forest wasn't logged in the past, there are a huge variety of trees including tulip tree, buckeye, basswood, silver bell, hemlock, sugar maple, and black cherry. These forests are typically below 4,500 feet.

Hemlock Forest: Typically found near stream and shady areas below 4,000 feet. Some of these forests are known to have huge eastern hemlock trees. Rhododendron are also found in this area.

Pine and Oak Forests: These forests are often on drier, exposed ridges. Fires are more common in these areas. Trees of this forest include oaks, pines, and mountain laurels.

"There's one!" he exclaimed.

Morgan came over to look with James.

Mom gazed at the dense tangle of trees overhead. "I like these lower forests much more," she announced. "It's nice and shady down here."

After their break, the Parkers continued to wind their way down. Soon, the trail merged with a gravel road. "We're getting close," Dad said.

They passed another cemetery. James, Morgan, Mom, and Dad walked to the edge of it.

Morgan recalled her dream. "Cemeteries and tombstones make me nervous."

"Let's keep going, then," Dad said.

The trail was level now, and followed another gurgling Smokies stream.

"There's a tent up ahead!" Morgan noticed.

They entered the campground. The Parkers found a campsite and set down their packs.

Mom sighed. "It's such a relief to take that off."

"I'll be right back," Dad said.

Dad walked off, but was back with the car a few minutes later. He found his family sprawled out on the benches and table at the campsite, barefoot and staring at the trees above.

Dad surveyed the scene. "I think I'll join you," he said, then limped over and lay down on the picnic table bench. "Now, that was a great hike!" he announced.

After dinner, Dad made some popcorn. The Parkers sat around and indulged.

"It's our last night in the Smokies," Morgan realized. "Just thinking of that makes me sad."

James sat up. "Mom, can you read the last page of Great-Grandpa's journal?"

"An excellent idea," Mom agreed. She fished through her pack, found her grandfather's journal, and opened it to the last entry. Mom quickly scanned the words. "Hmm, that's interesting."

"What?" Morgan asked.

"Well, this journal entry is dated years later—1955. But I'll read it anyway."

> *Max Davis here.*
>
> *I just spent several hours working in the garden of my San Luis Obispo, California, home...*

Mom stopped reading and looked up at her family. "I guess this last section isn't about the Smokies."

"Go on and read it anyway," Dad said.

> *I've just finished planting several shrubs in the side yard. I can't wait to see them when they're full grown. It's a little memorial garden for my days in the Great Smoky Mountains.*

Mom paused for a few seconds. "He's talking about the plants in our yard," Mom realized. "Grandpa was always so into gardening when he lived there."

"Please go on," James begged.

> *I planted some rhododendron. They grow abundantly in the Smokies. I hope they do well here too.*
>
> *So, if you've found this journal tucked away in my home and you've read*

these pages, now you know what I've planted and why I planted them. Please treat my memorial garden well.

    Sincerely,

    Max Davis

Mom took a deep breath and looked away.

Morgan looked at Mom. "You have tears in your eyes," Morgan said.

Dad put his arm around Mom and held her close.

"I guess Grandpa wanted someone to read his journal," Mom said. "I'm sure glad we did."

The Parkers sat quietly in their campsite with the campfire crackling away. The night sky slowly enveloped everything around them. Then, after a period of long silence, James slowly stood up. "I'll be right back."

James grabbed his flashlight and walked away. A few minutes later, he returned to his family. Morgan, Dad, and Mom were all sitting in the exact same spot, staring off into the dark woods.

James broke the silence. "Guess what?" he announced. "Those moths are still there."

Dad looked up. "Really? This time I want to see them."

"Me too," Mom said.

All four of the Parkers trekked over to the bathrooms. Mom and Morgan went into the women's room, James and Dad into the men's.

A few minutes later they met outside to tell each other what they saw and to exchange the camera. After that, they met back at camp.

With her family gathered around, Morgan flipped through pictures on the digital camera.

"I wonder if they were the same moths as last time," Morgan said.

"I don't know," James said, "but I really like that little peach-colored one with the red antennas. It's my favorite."

"You know what?" Dad said. "Let's buy an identification booklet at the visitor center on our way out. That way we'll know their names."

Dad flipped over pancakes on the camp stove, then looked at his tired family. "It's nice to sleep in for a change, isn't it?" he asked.

Morgan, Mom, and James nodded in agreement.

"Our flight isn't until tomorrow morning," Dad recalled. "And it's about four hours back to Nashville. So if we drive through the park today and do a little more sightseeing, we'll still make it to our hotel at a decent hour tonight."

"Sounds like a plan," Mom agreed.

The Parkers took Highway 321 west of Cosby. Once they passed through Gatlinburg, the Parkers stopped at the Sugarlands Visitor Center. They watched a movie about the park, chatted with a ranger about ticks at the information station, and walked around the museum. James stopped and stared at the massive hellbender on display. The incredibly large salamander was rusty brown with black dots. It had a flat head, a paddlelike tail, and little eyes.

Dad came up to James. "How would you like to run into one of those in a Smokies stream?"

James looked at Dad. "It would be *way cool*!"

Afterward, they drove west along Little River Road.

Dad turned the car north at a junction, and soon they reached the turnoff to Little Greenbrier School. Dad drove up the dirt road to the historic schoolhouse and parked the car there.

After exploring the school, the Parkers walked up to a gate blocking a gravel road. A sign there read Walker Cabin 1.1 miles.

"This is it!" Dad announced.

The Parkers walked silently up the road. *I wonder if this is the same trail the Walker sisters took to school every day,* Morgan thought.

"You know," Mom recalled, "the ranger mentioned that there used to be a sign near the school encouraging people to visit the Walker sisters. They would even make gifts for the tourists who came."

"That's what they did for Great-Grandpa, they gave him a gift!" Morgan said.

They continued walking, crossing a small stream along the way. The Parkers turned a bend in the trail and forged ahead. Soon there was a clearing. Right in the middle of it was an old rustic cabin.

Once at the Walker sisters' cabin, Morgan, James, Mom, and Dad wandered around.

Mom walked into the yard. She noticed patterns of rocks and plants that indicated where a garden had once been. "This yucca and cedar certainly don't look native," she said, "and neither do these old hedges."

Dad walked over to the shed. Old rusty tools were hanging near a workbench. Then Dad wandered to the springhouse. He noticed a man-made rock waterway that channeled right under the structure. "Ingenious," Dad muttered. "Water directed for refrigeration, just like Grandpa said."

James looked up at the rock chimney, then stepped onto the porch. He put his foot on a wooden bench to test how sturdy it was. A moment later, James went into the cabin. He passed by Morgan and found the stairs to the loft. James climbed the stairs and explored the second story of the home.

Morgan walked slowly around the cabin's main floor. She noticed remnant pieces of magazine and newspaper clippings used for wallpaper. Morgan took a close look at some of the torn and faded clippings, but they were too old to read. She saw an old dishpan, and there were nails for hanging utensils. Then she meandered over to the fireplace.

"I can totally picture the Walker sisters living here," Morgan said out loud. *And in many ways, I already have,* she realized.

Morgan explored some more. She looked through the windows of the cabin and saw her parents outside. James was now out there too. He was peering underneath some rocks and boxwood bushes.

Morgan strolled back into the living room.

She stared at the fireplace, imagining a warm, crackling fire. Then Morgan pictured the whole cabin full of life. There were antique rocking chairs, a stove, various cooking utensils, and a pad of paper. A rifle was resting against the wall. Morgan added the five Walker sisters to the scene.

Each of the sisters was working. Martha was churning butter in a large jar with a lid. Polly was sewing a blanket. Hettie was nailing a hook on the wall. Louisa was writing poetry in her journal. And Margaret was sitting in a chair, warmly looking at Morgan, while she peeled apples.

"We're glad you came," Margaret said to Morgan. "Sit down, and don't mind our organized confusion."

Morgan sat on the floor, pretending it was a chair. "Somebody has to pass on our legacy and tell our story," Margaret said. "And I think you are a great person to do that."

Morgan closed her eyes and concentrated, trying to soak in every word. "By the way," Margaret added, "we really enjoyed your great-grandfather's visits."

That surprised Morgan. She opened her eyes and looked up. Now there were only two sisters left, Louisa and Margaret, both much older. They sat gently in their chairs, calm and relaxed.

"We really can't take visitors anymore," Louisa explained. "It's just too much work for us. We told them to take down the sign."

Morgan looked at the two elderly women. "I understand," she pretended to say. Morgan closed her eyes again, then opened them. Now there was only Louisa, who was rocking slowly in her chair, looking frail and old.

"Don't forget about us," Louisa spoke her final words to Morgan. "Or else the mystery of the park's history will be lost."

"Morgan!" Dad called from outside.

Dad's voice snapped Morgan out of her daydream. She quickly jumped to her feet and walked toward the cabin's front door. Morgan paused to look around one more time. "Good-bye, Walker sisters," Morgan said out loud to the empty cabin. Then she turned around and joined her family.

Mom and Dad were standing next to James by a circle of rocks surrounding several plants. James bent down. "There's a rabbit under here," he announced.

The small rabbit bounded out from underneath the plants and ran across the open, grassy area. It came to the tall, denser grass near some trees and stopped. The rabbit looked at the Parkers with its nose twitching.

"Great-Grandpa did say the Walker sisters had rabbits around," Morgan recalled, "so that one might be one of their kids."

"Or grandkids," James chimed in.

"Or great-grandkids," Morgan added.

The Parkers stood quietly. "How long do rabbits usually live, anyway?" Dad finally said.

After a few more minutes at the Walker Cabin, Mom, Dad, Morgan, and James strolled back to their car at the Little Greenbrier School.

"There's the Chimney picnic area," Morgan said.

Dad turned the car into the parking lot. James and Mom got out.

"We'll pick you up here in two and a half hours," Dad reminded them.

Morgan and Dad drove away.

"Two and a half hours," Dad repeated. "That will really test our hiking ability."

• • •

James and Mom gathered with a group of people. "Welcome, everyone," a ranger spoke. "My name is Mark. This is the Junior Ranger salamander program, where we get to do one of the coolest things you can do in the Smokies. Follow me, and get ready to get wet and slimy!"

• • •

Dad parked the car at the nearby Chimney Tops trailhead. Morgan and Dad quickly got out. They hurried to the trail and began hiking. After crossing several footbridges over roaring Smokies streams, Morgan and Dad began to climb.

The trail quickly became steep. Morgan and Dad worked hard to keep up their pace. The pathway, like many in the Smokies, was full of wet roots and slippery rocks. At times there were cables to help them with their footing. Dad wiped the sweat off his brow and took a deep breath. "I'm sure glad I'm in great shape," he joked.

• • •

Mark propped one of his feet up on a rock near a stream. "Believe it or not," he exclaimed, "this whole area is teeming with salamanders, and we get to find some."

Mom and James looked at each other.

Mark held up a small plastic container. "We'll temporarily display the salamanders in these. But please remember where you find them so they can be returned to their exact home."

James raised his hand. "What if we catch a hellbender?"

• • •

Morgan and Dad continued climbing. Up ahead a series of large roots completely covered the trail. "The plants are so fascinating here," Dad commented.

They stepped over the roots and approached a large, charcoal gray rock formation. Dad peered up at the massive, slanted rock. "I guess that's the Chimney Tops," he announced. "You can really see how the crust of the Earth buckled and tilted in this area."

Dad started climbing and Morgan followed. They took several steps, propelling themselves upward by grabbing the natural holds in the rock.

After several more steps, Dad and Morgan stopped. They stood there, halfway up the Chimney Tops. Dad looked up at the steep climb ahead of them. "I wonder if we should go on."

• • •

Mark smiled at James's question. "We would be extremely lucky to see one," he said emphatically. "I've been working here for nearly twenty years, and I've only seen a hellbender once. But I know they're out there. Hellbenders live in the larger streams in the lower valleys. Still, even in the rivers, the hellbender is awfully elusive.

"If you do find a salamander," he continued, "try to touch it as little as possible. And don't just look near the water. Try moving rocks, old bark, or logs, or even try looking under leaves and twigs."

• • •

Morgan and Dad scrambled farther up the slanted gray rock. They scanned the horizon. Across the way was a large, bulging mountain. "Mount LeConte," Dad observed. Morgan and Dad gazed out over the dense, seemingly impenetrable forest. Wisps of mist and clouds hovered over the valley. Far below was Newfound Gap Road. They could hear the traffic humming, even as far away as they were.

"Mom would really love seeing the forest from up here," Morgan said.

Dad surveyed the rest of their climb. "I wonder how the holds are up there."

"The holds?" Morgan asked.

"I mean how safe it will be for us to grab onto and climb up that rock."

Dark, ominous clouds drifted overhead. A faint rumble rolled in the distance.

• • •

"I got one!" James called out. He carefully picked up the small, yellowish, orange-striped salamander and put it into his plastic dish. James stood up and walked toward Mark, showing the salamander to Mom along the way.

Mark looked in the dish. "A Blue Ridge two-lined salamander!" he stated with enthusiasm. "Where did you find it?"

"Under that downed log," James pointed out.

"Good find," Mark said. "Here, put it at the front of our display table."

James put the salamander down and trotted off to search for more.

• • •

Morgan and Dad took a few more slow, cautious steps toward the summit of the Chimney Tops. The sky had grown darker, and a few large raindrops began to plunk down.

Dad sensed something unusual about the air. He heard a faint humming sound. Dad quickly looked around. Then he saw some of Morgan's hair sticking straight up.

Dad grabbed Morgan. "Duck!" he shouted.

Dad and Morgan immediately crouched down. Dad covered both their heads.

A blast of light illuminated the air. It was instantly followed by deafening thunder.

Once the thunder stopped, Dad peeked up. "I think the top of this rock might have been hit."

"Chimney Tops?" Morgan asked.

"Let's get out of here," Dad said urgently, "before lightning strikes it again."

Morgan and Dad scrambled to their feet. The rain picked up, and the slippery rock quickly became soaked. Morgan squinted her eyes and glanced at the sky. Lightning lit the clouds again, followed by booming thunder.

• • •

James, Mom, and the others continued searching. "There are eighteen salamanders and seven different species up here so far," Mark announced.

Mom walked up with a black-colored salamander adorned with reddish cheeks. "I found it under some leaves," Mom said.

Mark's eyes lit up. "The famous red-cheeked salamander!" he exclaimed. "It only lives in the Smokies. Excellent!"

Suddenly the sky let loose. Rain showered on the trees above the group. Large drops of water plunked down from the forest. Everyone looked at Mark, wondering what to do.

"Let's keep searching," Mark called out. "It's perfect salamander weather!"

• • •

Morgan and Dad quickly scrambled down from the rock. They reached the bottom and dashed down the trail, heading for the protection of the trees.

They got under a large tree and huddled together.

Dad felt his soaked visor. He got out the parkas and they slipped them on just as thunder rumbled again.

Morgan and Dad stepped out from under the tree and rain poured down on them. They started working their way back down the trail.

• • •

Mark gathered the group in front of the salamander display. He pointed and said, "A blackbelly over here. A tiny pygmy salamander here. Here's your red-cheeked and your Blue Ridge two-lined." He looked at James and Mom. "And, we have a shovelnose and also this southern redback. Great finds, everyone."

After putting their salamanders back, the parents and children started leaving. Eventually, only Mom and James were left.

"Our car isn't here," James informed Mark. "My dad and sister are still hiking."

"That's okay," Mark said. "Let's put your salamanders back and do a little more searching while we wait." Mark opened a large umbrella and motioned for Mom and James to get under it. "We aren't salamanders, you know," he joked.

Mom and James returned their salamanders to where they'd found them. Then they followed Mark to the stream.

• • •

Morgan and Dad kept hiking, but the Smokies storm was drenching them.

Dad wiped the water off his watch to get a quick glimpse at the time. "Getting there late is better than not at all," he said to Morgan.

Suddenly Dad slipped, tumbling down a wet, muddy embankment. He tried to get up, but his foot slipped out from under him. He fell back into the mud on the steep slope. Morgan carefully stepped off the trail and gave Dad a hand. Together they were able to pull him back onto his feet.

Dad looked at himself and smirked. "Now I know what it's like to wallow like a salamander."

• • •

Mark pointed to the water. "What hellbenders really like," he explained, "is to hide under rocks in big pools of water." Mark gazed at the large pool ahead of them. "Like this one."

Mom and James also looked at the creek.

"Usually the people who get to see hellbenders are those who come out with snorkeling gear and go underwater," Mark explained. Then he looked up at the weather. "And I don't think we want to do that today."

Mom nodded. "I can understand why."

They heard the sound of squishing footsteps coming down the trail.

Mom and James looked up.

Morgan was standing there in a totally soaked red parka. Dad's orange parka was completely caked with wet, dripping mud.

Mom and James thanked Mark and walked up to Morgan and Dad. "Are you okay?" James asked.

Dad smiled sheepishly. "Yes."

James looked at Dad and grinned. "You look like a giant salamander!" he announced.

Dad bared his white teeth and growled. "Yep. Call me the hellbender!"

Any salamanders around?

Well here we are, back at the Quiet Walkway next to the river.

I'm sad that my vacation in the Smokies is almost over. But I hope you enjoyed reading about our adventures.

So let me bring you back to exactly where we left off.

James just called out urgently, "Hey, you guys, come here!"

We quickly walked over to James, who stood by the river. "I saw one!" he exclaimed. "It's in there."

"What is?" I asked.

"A hellbender!"

We looked at the river, but it was getting too dark to see under the water.

James scanned the riverbank and went to grab a stick.

He took the stick and propped it underneath a rock, hoisting it up a few inches.

The hellbender dashed out and quickly glided along the river bottom. "There it is!" I shouted.

The enormous amphibian gracefully propelled itself right under a larger rock and disappeared. "Unbelievable," Mom exclaimed.

James took a deep, satisfied breath. "At least we got to see it for a second."

"Yep, the old waterdog," Dad commented. "It was huge!"

"Waterdog," James repeated, looking at Dad in his muddy orange parka. Dad glanced at his clothes. "Me?"

James smiled. "Maybe that can be your new nickname!"

Dad looked thoughtful. "I'm not sure if I like that," he said. Then he noticed the darkening skies. "Come on, everyone, we've got a lot of driving ahead, and I know we're all looking forward to a hotel, clean clothes, and a shower."

Dad put his arms around James and me. We all started walking back to the car.

Suddenly, somewhere in the forest, a tiny group of lights sparkled brightly for several seconds, then just as quickly disappeared. The lights sparkled again, this time closer to us.

We stopped in our tracks and looked at each other silently, as if each of us was saying, "Did you see what I just saw?"

Another group of lights twinkled away in a different part of the forest.

Finally, Mom spoke. "Fireflies," she gasped. "Only they're doing something I've never heard of. They're lighting in sync with each other."

"It looks like a miniature Christmas light parade," I said.

We stood still and watched the Great Smoky Mountain Firefly Show.

SPARKING IN SYNC

There are fourteen species of fireflies in Great Smoky Mountains National Park. Fireflies use a process called bioluminescence, a chemical reaction made by living things to produce their own light. Synchronous fireflies are uncommon in North America. They were hardly known about until 1994, when they were discovered in the Elkmont area of the park. Scientists aren't certain why fireflies spark in sync. Some believe that males do this to compete with each other. They want to be the first spark to attract females. Another idea is that males light up in unison because the more light there is, the better their chances of being noticed by a female. Today, synchronous fireflies are one of the most famous attractions in the Smokies. Peak synchronous firefly viewing occurs in the Elkmont area for a two-week period each June.

The fireflies kept lighting up in groups throughout the forest. "There are hundreds of them," James called out.

"And a bunch more over here," I added, looking in another direction.

"It's quite a grand finale we're seeing here," Dad commented.

Mom looked at her watch. "Wow, 9 p.m.," she realized. "We really better get going."

• • •

Several hours later we were on Highway 40 heading west to Nashville. It was around midnight. Mom and Dad were up front. James and I were in back, staring out the window. An occasional, solitary firefly sparkled in the bushes next to the freeway. We had been seeing them for hours now.

"I wish we had them in California," I said to James.

Then my thoughts drifted back home.

It was sometime in the future. James and I had just fertilized the rhododendron that Great-Grandpa had planted years ago, when he lived where we live now. I wish I could have met him. We might have worked on the garden together. But in some ways, we are now.

I was dousing the base of the plants with water. "It just doesn't rain as much here as in the Smokies," I explained to James.

James looked at me. "You know what I think we should call this garden?"

"What?"

"The GGG—for Great-Grandpa's Garden."

I turned away from James and saw another speck of light as our car zipped by on the freeway. Lightning lit up the clouds. To anyone who reads this journal in the future, take my advice and please go to the Great Smoky Mountains. They are fantastic!

What do I recommend that you see? Well, here's my Top Ten List of favorite sights:

1. The Walker sisters cabin and Little Greenbrier School
2. Cataloochee Valley Historic Area
3. Synchronized fireflies!
4. Abrams Falls
5. Mount LeConte and Mount LeConte Lodge
6. The Chimney Tops
7. Clingmans Dome
8. Cosby Campground moths
9. Charlies Bunion
10. The AT Trail and shelters

My brother James says he would add these sights:

11. Jr. Ranger salamander program
12. Andrews Bald
13. Cades Cove bike ride
14. Newfound Gap
15. The hellbender!
16. Rainbow Falls
17. Place of a Thousand Drips
18. Elk in Cataloochee

After talking with the ranger at the Sugarlands Visitor Center, my parents think I had tick paralysis. When the tick is stuck on someone, it releases toxins, making the person feel sick and sore. But once the tick is removed, people recover quickly, just like I did.

It's raining now, and the car's windshield wipers are slapping back and forth. As I watch the driving night storm, I see bright lights and tall buildings ahead.

"The Nashville skyline!" Dad exclaims, and I know this trip is over...